Introduction

Owing to endless decades of wars and
insignificant hatred of blacks b-
divide and rule, a medieval Afr.
young black children resident in   _in
about being gratefully black. The   , the
children back in time to forewarn ,   .u queens about
the grand corruption *Innocent* white ,   ,erpetrate in Africa
today; the irrelevance of today's Africans abroad to the economic,
security development of the continent and the general
indiscriminate disrespect to black lives in other that they may
have rethinking about accepting *Innocent* white guests of those
days.

Contents

Chapter one.
Tuesday 7th April 2020
Ikeja, Lagos.
AJOSE'S FAMILY

8:40 pm
Korede: "So, because I yell at you when you do something wrong,
then whenever you're going on an errand to shop, you'll be
walking as if you're someone dejected, walking sluggishly and
tired. Some woman in the neighborhood said she saw my house-

3

girl, and she isn't looking good. I rebuked her, I told her I don't have a house-girl, that they're both my daughters. You're my daughter whether you like it or not. So, if you like to hang your neck like a turkey; I can't do anything about your case anymore. By the way, what do you want me to do? If I buy you clothes you'll not wear; if I suggest a style of dress, you'll say you don't like it. I know how many dresses my husband has bought for you that you leave to suffocate in your locker. Just small talk I'll talk, you'll hang your shoulders like someone agonized. See, me I lived with my aunt before I got married and I smacked her children deservedly; but that was then. I know the tricks of babysitting. My dear, me I want you to understand that I won't allow you smack my children. Isn't that what causes us to fight? Madam Kate, I'm talking to you. My aunt's children were very rude but mine are respectful. Let's stop having problems with this. Did their daddy phone in? Kate, I'm talking to you, did their daddy call?"

Kate: "No ma! He didn't phone in."

Korede: "Answer me na! If I'm talking, please answer me."

Kate: "I said no ma! You didn't hear me."

Korede: "So I'm deaf abi!"

Kate: "No ma!" Salau pushes the door and lets himself into the room.

"Mummy my neck is hurting me." Salau said as he, hopping on the bed, went and wrapped his mother from behind, placing his right ear against her back.

Korede: "My love, come here. Sorry dear, maybe you placed your body weight on your neck while you slept."

Salau: "No mummy, it's Hafeez that will be pushing me when he's sleeping; he doesn't know how to sleep." Korede turns one hundred and eighty degrees and gathers Salau in her arms to embrace him and plants a kiss on his head. She's also committed to finishing Kate's hair she was braiding.

Korede: "But why do you always sleep on his bed?"

Salau: "No mummy, he's the one that comes to my bed. He won't listen when I tell him to lie on his bed."

Korede: "So, if you like when next you're going to shop, don't smile like a happy beautiful girl should, that's your business. If

4

you like to listen, If you like to keep that your face anyway you please, my own is just keep your head well lemme finish this hair I'm braiding; my back is hurting me."

Korede Ajose (née Ariwokamni) is the mother of Tinuke, Salau and Hafeez in her seventeenth year of marriage and wife to Olamilekan Ajose. She is an aide worker with WindCity Initiatives, an action group funded by the General Union primarily for the protection and general wellbeing of the girl-child. She is sitting on the bed weaving the hair of her maidservant, Kate, who is sitting on a wooden stool backing Korede and facing the window in a room upstairs in her matrimonial duplex which has three more rooms. Kate Ndope is the daughter of Kella and Doris Ndope, both farmers from Benue state; she was accepted by the Ajoses' when she was six years old in other to ease low-income Kella Ndope the burden of funding her growth and a promise to raise her until she attained higher education level in consideration of Kate assisting with house chores. She is currently awaiting results of the junior *waec* she sat for. Kate loves watching and listening to traditional African dramas and songs.

9:20 pm
Salau: "Mummy, where's daddy?"
Korede: "I don't know, call him."
Salau: "Where's your phone? I don't have airtime."
Korede: "Use Kate's own, he won't answer mine. Kate, where is your phone?"
Kate: "Ma, I don't have airtime."
Korede: "Will you ever say you have? Salau, look over there, bring my purse, my small phone is in there, let me transfer airtime to Kate."
Salau: "Which one?"
Korede: "That brown one; no, is that one brown?; okay bring that one you're holding, bring that other one you held up! No, no not that one. Just bring it like that; yes bring them, that one... Yes! Thank you. Simple color you don't know, is this brown? This is chestnut. I don't know what they teach you people these days in school- wait! Where is your brother?"

5

Salau: "He's sleeping."

Korede: "Go and check; sorry. Just help me check on him. Don't be angry, my love, my husband. Madam Kate, what is that your number again?"

Kate: "Hmmm! Aunty, I'm owing them five hundred o!"

Korede: "How come? See this girl o! You're not working nor earning, you're taking loans. By the way, who are you calling with your airtime?"

Kate: "I called my mummy."

Korede: "So, it's every time, every time, you're calling her?"

Kate: "No, I was missing her. When I see you and Hafeez and Salau, I start missing her."

Korede: "Okay o! *Oya*, call your number."

Salau: "He's still sleeping."

Korede: "Thank you love. *Oya* take, it's ringing."

Salau: "Hello daddy, where are you? You bought me yoghurt? Yoghurt and *suya*? Thank you daddy. Hafeez is sleeping. Should I wake him up? I love you daddy." Salau runs out of his parents room and into he's and his younger brother's room to wake him up.

"Hafeez! Hafeez!" Salau shook him aggressively. "Daddy bought a PS4 for you!" The honk of a car is heard, Salau recognizes that sound and dashing out the room door, toward the staircase, he got to the premises gate barefoot in spider-man pajamas shortly after the gatekeeper, Usman had opened the black color sliding gate. Salau rushed the right front and rear doors knob of the 2012 car, pulling them multiple times while the car slowly rolled into the compound before it halted. The trunk of the car popped, it pulled Salau to it, he threw off the booth and reached for a carton of PS4 which was packed with other items he didn't bother about. He's gasping for air, he carefully, but hastily returns to the house. He went straight to the living room and settled in the presence of a seventy-two inch television that hung on the wall. He's pulling out wires, white ones, red and yellow wires and plugging the same on the right end of the TV set while screaming Hafeez on the top of his voice.

9:55 pm

Salau and his brother Hafeez are in the living room unpacking the console and are trying to connect the wires appropriately to the television set, and or searching for a channel on the TV set, which weren't coming to futility.

"Babe I didn't even think you're home, I didn't see you downstairs; where's your car?" Olamilekan said when he entered his room. "I asked Sa, he didn't even answer me." He added.
"Ten o'clock in the night, where would I be? I'm making Kate's hair; my car is in the mechanic's workshop." Korede replied.
Kate: "Good evening sir."
"Kate, how are you?" Olamilekan inquired of her.
"Fine, thank you sir, welcome." Kate responded.
"Thank you. Better person; my own wife didn't even welcome me." He teased.
"The people that came back from work, we've told them welcome." Korede said, still braiding Kate's hair. Salau pushes himself into the room.
Salau: "Daddy come and fix the game for me."
Korede: "Fix what for you? Will you go and sleep, see the time."
Salau: "Daddy come and fix it for me, please."
Korede: "I said go to your room."
Salau: "Leave me alone! Daddy!" He starts to cry.
"Babe take it easy, he's with me." Olamilekan adds his voice.
"It's to-ten and they ought to be in bed. They have been up since six o'clock in the morning." Korede insisted and this drew a louder cry from Salau. He walks out angrily to his room.
Olamilekan: "But it's twelve noon he's to resume, he can play for another one hour."
Korede: "I know, but how will Hafeez sleep if Salau is awake?"
Olamilekan: "Kilode to shey ma'n soro egbin simi, to' de ri pe omo yi wa'n biyi? O'ni owo fun mi, bo ti le je wipe awon eyan wa ni bi"
Korede: "Mi'o soro egbin si e. Pa pa, Omo na o'gbo Yoruba."
Olamilekan: "Kate, go to your room."

Korede: "No, I'm finishing her hair tonight, because I'm taking Hafeez to the hospital tomorrow, I won't be able to make her hair and I can't leave her looking older than my mother."

Olamilekan: "Why, what's wrong with Hafeez? Why didn't you even tell me my boy is ill? We're in this same room together."

Korede: "You're not always around when they need you, you're out there making money for your family. He's had runny noses and he's got heat packed up inside him. He's feverish too and has refused to eat anything."

Olamilekan: "Have you called Ovie?"

Korede: "No, I texted him."

Olamilekan: "He's not going to school tomorrow."

Korede: "No, he's not. But I haven't taken permission from work just yet."

Hafeez was left all alone in the living room, Salau went to get help earlier to connect the game console to the television and then cried to sleep after his mother insisted he went to bed. Kate's hair was completed; she proceeded to sleep because of a sprain. Her neck hurt due to how she sat for hours on when her hair was braided. Mr and Mrs Ajose argued for a while and slept off.

Wednesday 8th April, 2020
3:00 am
Olamilekan got up and went downstairs to the living room and found Hafeez sitting, sleeping on the couch-facing the television, neck tilted left side, one control-pad on his thighs, another on his left side. The television set was on, same as the game console, he noticed two extra adventure game CDs he didn't bring home. The window was open and the air conditioner was switched on. He closed the window, turned off the air conditioner and carried Hafeez upstairs to his room with Salau. His body was quite hot and he was talking in his sleep.

Olamilekan placed Hafeez on his bed and covered his lower body with the duvet. Switched off the light, then shut the door as he left. A couple of minutes after, Hafeez got out of his bed, eyes shut and went over to Salau's bed and touched his toes severally. Then he went back to sleep, covering himself just the way his father did. Salau stood up, eyes shut and went to the window and opened it. Standing there, he's staring into the distance with both eyes closed.

Chapter two.
Wednesday 8th April, 2020

Surulere, Lagos.
UMAHI'S FAMILY

6:57 am
"Mummy!" Emeka called out a second time. "Mummy Ejike doesn't want to bathe." He added, "Ejike, if I come and meet you there!" Aniete said from the kitchen. It was the third day of resumption for primary schools across the country and the final stage of easing the lockdown. However secondary schools had resumed weeks earlier. States of federation have devised separate techniques to reduce the spread of the virus while waiting for a vaccine. There was still some getting used to after over eight months of total and partial lockdown to curtail the spread of the rampaging virus.
"Ejike, if I smack you! Will you allow him to clean you up? Every time it's for school, you'll start feeling sick... Come here!" Aniete was saying, almost whispering. She grabbed the five year old male from the bathroom and into the boys room and wiped his body dry, creamed and dressed him.
"Emeka, go out and tell them Ejike is coming. Just wait by the bus and don't say anything else." There came Aniete, running out with Ejike's lunchbox and school bag approaching a waiting school bus. Ejike is walking majestically behind his mother, hands in his pockets, shirt tucked in with a matching bow-tie; looking gorgeous.

Aniete Umahi, (née Ekpenyong) an employee of a private secondary school worker, owned by her in-laws and a red-cross volunteer, mother of Udoka, 16, Emeka, 8 and Ejika, 5, and widow of Chukwubuike Umahi got a phone call from the police in Area K division over a complaint against her son regarding threats to life and property in his school. She phoned her brother-in-law and intimated him. Boarding two buses to the almost three kilometers police station Aniete demanded to see Udoka, whom they provided.
Aniete: "Udo what happened? Are you alright? What did they do to you?"
Udoka: "Mummy, I'm fine. I'm okay!"

The visitor's section in the juvenile justice department of the state police was a large space demarcated with sound-proof walls to temporarily allow for three or maybe four persons including the juvenile. A three storey structure was donated to the police force by a family who responded to a need for thorough sophistication in the police station following an incident where a mid-ranked police officer was nursing his ill son and had him stay over in the station as he wasn't fit for school that sad day, while he did some administrative work. The final report of the incident had it that there was a child who suffered a disorder at an infant age, picked up a loaded pistol, his dads', from the pistol holding and started shooting at everyone. Killing his dad along with two other officers; a few others sustained injuries. The child was shot at to neutralize him, eventually dying at the hospital.

"Did you steal anything?" Aniete squeezed Udoka, sitting in a demarcated enclosed space.

"No mom, I didn't. They're just mad I refused them from searching my locker. Mom, imagine they told us not to resume camp with phones or other devices, and someone is complaining of missing phones. Aren't they supposed to ignore him? It's okay for contraband to go missing. It's not supposed to be there in the first place." Udoka replied, a stern look gripped his face.

"In other words, we wouldn't be here if you had opened your locker for them to peep through since the phone in question isn't there? Answer me." Aniete said, taking deep breaths.

"Yes mom!" Udoka replied.

"Oh my goodness! What manner of disrespect did you display to the whole school?" She starts yelling, raising her voice prematurely. "Was your principal there?" She added, "Yes mom." He replied. "Udoka, what have you done? Do you know what you have done?" She whispered.

"Mom you won't understand. They all had this 'I stole it' look on their faces from the get go. Mom lemme tell you, they're just trying to make sure I don't make the team for the National games. They're so mad I was voted captain by the majority of students that elected to vote that day." Udoka said, not giving into pressure to wrongdoing.

"What makes you so sure it's because of the National games?" Aniete inquired into his allegation.

"They're jealous! What else can I say? Mom, my favorite position is right-wing-back, even the grass on the pitch knows that, and Kola and I are the favorites in that position. Now Coachie and team managers settled for me to play right-flank knowing I'm not very fast. Regardless of the politics, my training ratio, ball control, stamina and fitness level is higher than Obed, Malik, James; even Jasper *sef* that they're calling Messi, he's not that better than me to be honest. They say that if I must be allowed to participate from a previous set, I'm not eligible for captaincy." He replied.

Aniete: "Must you be captain? Isn't this all for a possible spot in the Olympics and other top competitions? What's the captaincy desire for anyways?"

Udoka: "I didn't nominate myself, I didn't vote for myself."

"When are the National games starting?" Aniete asked,

"Exactly four months today." He answered,

"Should I talk with your Coach?" Aniete said,

"No mom. Don't tell him anything, don't tell anyone anything, I got this. I have a point I want to prove to a few people in school." He said, his eyes are getting wet, gathering teardrops. A while later, Udoka is shedding tears, sobbing. Then wiping tears rolling down his eyes, and then rubbing her thumb and palm of her hands on her Ankara dress she said, "Now son, be careful and do not be arrogant and proud. Just do all you can to get to the team, I know how long you've waited for this; and if it wasn't for the lockdown..." "Yeah mom," he interrupted her, "if it wasn't for the lockdown I'd have gone to the festival last year. They postponed everything and now see what uncle Emma is saying that 'you don't have automatic right to the team for the National games because this is not your set. And that this set has more than enough talent to make the games' he's keeping his mouth like a fool!" Udoka said disgustingly about the insensitive process of selecting students to compete for a place in the National Sports Festival also known as National games.

"Now what did I tell you about cursing? Who are you calling a fool?" Aniete rebuked him.

"I'm sorry mom." He replied.

12

"Learn to control your tongue!"

The investigating police officer assigned to the incident interrupted the session between Aniete and Udoka.

IPO: "Madam, you're free to go with your son. An incident was reported over intimidation and threat to life by your son and we were invited to arrest the situation. After investigators carried out their work we realized that this young man was unjustly accused of stealing a device. And we have sought apology from the parties to your son here, for the unruly things they reported against him. From our investigations, your son is a usual suspect having been in or around thefts of more than six items; or knowing persons who have been caught with stolen items since this year's academic training sessions began; that is quite a feat."

Aniete: "Are you indirectly telling me that my son was arrested and detained because of past events that some of the accounts, just like this one, were even found to have been false or unjustly attempting to discredit my son?"

IPO: "No Ma, I'm outrightly saying you both can go home."

Aniete: "No, you haven't heard the last of me."

IPO: "Madam, I said we were informed of threats made by your son, not because an item was stolen. It was at the scene that we were informed of a missing phone which escalated quickly into threats being made. And upon the end of the investigation, we arrived at the conclusion that he wasn't the person that stole the phone."

Aniete: "Contraband? Was it supposed to be there in the first place?"

IPO: "Certainly not ma, as a matter of fact, that student has been expelled from the institution."

Udoka: "Wow!"

Aniete: 'I see! That said, we'll leave immediately." And she started gathering her items into her hand bag.

IPO: "Young man, control your temper."

Udoka: "Okay sir."

They left the station and hopped on several busses until they arrived at Agege, the location of the school, NEWLAND high school. Upon reaching the school's main gate, Aniete started fuming; disgust was written all over her. Regardless, she was made to undergo a body temperature check, and use hand sanitizer. Her face-mask was worn properly. She asked for the principal and then the form-mistress. She expressed her disappointment over the manner her son was labeled a thief and demanded an apology which the school authorities responded to having been sent out to be published in two local newspapers.

In the end, a letter was handed to Udoka disqualifying him from participating in the National games for causing disturbances in the hostel, threatening to beat up school security and total insubordination.

He starts crying.

"Oh c'com sir, he's just a kid, why are you taking this kind of harsh measure on a sixteen year old; this could be demoralizing for him. This could be your son or daughter; would this be your resolve?" Aniete said, as water filled her eyes.

"Disciplinary action against an athlete shouldn't be perceived as wicked. The ultimate idea is to correct the athlete and instill mannerism." The principal responded. Kneeling down, Aniete pleaded with the principal for the disqualification to be reviewed, that he acted like a teenager would when accused of something he didn't do. That was the cause of the entire incident. Aniete is bargaining, she's crying already.

"Had he obeyed simple instructions to allow the school security to check his locker there wouldn't have been any aggression." Principal added.

"He was standing by his rights?" Aniete mentions,

"Being disobedient? Obedience is cherished more than sacrifice. Also madam, after reviewing the comments by the school's guardian and counselor, Mrs Igbokwe, we noticed that there might have been traits of both physical and mental abuse on your son at a younger age, as we sensed that might have been where he got his anger from. He gets upset easily." The principal added.

"I don't understand sir." Aniete said,

Principal: "I mean there may have been a period in his life when he was beaten as punitive measures, or for some other reason at all. If I'm correct, it may have definitely affected his behavior. It's about behavior, behavior is the repetition of activity to become a pattern, a way of life, or a style, if you may. Imagine when someone displays a behavior depicting he or she has been denied access to truth or justice or even fairness, they tend to take to violence and use of force to get that which they fear they might constantly lose. Not in all cases, yes but perhaps."

Aniete: "Yes sir, I must admit. My late husband had a principle of smacking him whenever he did anything wrong as a means of correcting him. My late husband was raised with iron-hands and he believed that males were to be brought up that way, he argued that it made them tough and ready for the wicked world. That aside, this boy just lost his dad. I'm still in shock, they're still in shock- my children. Him getting offended easily can be traced back to some fatal occurrences. Sir, I can tell about the effect the total lockdown had on him personally. In those days I couldn't afford data for them to browse, you could see they were about to implode. But they kept it cool with me. Please sir, I'm his mother, I know he's not a bad boy, he took it too far and I assure you, he won't do it again."

Principal: "Madam please take a seat. Don't make your son feel smacking, beating is the only form of punishment for disobedience or to learn how to face the world. He needs to know that in some instances, sanctions, deprivations, restrictions are other forms of punishing disobedience not necessarily flogging, beating or physically assaulting him. In beating a child, or just anyone, you are unleashing an animal who will comfortably know beating as the only form of punishment for disobeying orders. He'll know and encourage beating as dealing appropriately with misbehavior. Please stop it, stop tampering with his self esteem. The victim of his madness someday could be you or his wife in old age, or his siblings and classmates. We need gentlemen and women, not violence in human form."

Aniete: "Thank you sir, well noted sir." She wipes her wet eyes and rubs her palms on the sides of her dress. Her face-mask is wet with sweat and tears. "May I make one last request?" She added, "Of course!" The principal said,

Aniete: "That the disqualification of my son be reviewed and may he be allowed to participate in the qualifying round like every

other student and given a fair chance to prove himself worthy or not to represent his school. That's all I ask, sir."
Principal: "I'll look into it."

Chapter three.
Wednesday 8 April, 2020
Ikeja, Lagos
HAFEEZ AND HIS FRIEND

6:40 am
Olamilekan staggered into his sons room early in the morning with sleepy eyes to get Salau and maybe Hafeez ready for the day. He loved to wake them up early. Upon entering their room he found them up and fully dressed for school. Amazed, he quizzed them.
Hafeez: "Good morning dad!"
Olamilekan:"Good morning, what happened here?"
Hafeez: "We're ready for school."
Olamilekan: "I can see that. Hafeez you brushed your teeth?"
Hafeez: "It's white as snow, my teacher won't even know it's me talking." Hafeez opened his mouth wide and released a fresh minty breath.
Olamilekan: "I know, I said who made that possible?"
Hafeez: "Salau and I!"
"Korede come o! Something has entered these children." He yelled out to his wife. "Korede!" He called out louder.

"What is it?" Korede responds at the door of the room, still wiping her wet hands on her night-gown, followed shortly by Kate who stood outside the door peeping in.

"Repeat yourself!" Olamilekan said to Hafeez, a four year old.

Hafeez: "We said no need bothering mummy to cut short her sleep over and over again. So we decided to get ourselves ready. Ain't that right Sa?"

Salau: "Absolutely true!"

Korede:"Hmmm! See this one, who told you I'm bothered; and who knotted your tie?" Pointing at Salau. "And who said you're going to school today?" Referring to Hafeez.

Korede: "Ah! Salau what happened? Kate didn't wash those stockings; Ola something happened here."

Hafeez: "C'mon mom, we'll be late for school."

Salau: "Daddy, we've got work to do at school."

Olamilekan and Korede bundled the boys into the car and headed to the hospital in Ikeja. Korede was certain Hafeez had a cold, but these weren't nightmares. As Olamilekan drove, both of them in the front seats pondered what could have come over their sons. Their thoughts run wild.

They arrived early and their doctor friend, Ovie Donald, hadn't arrived at the hospital. The boys were asleep in the back seat of the car and they remained in the car with their mother while Olamilekan went to the consultant ward to get a hospital-card and get them an impromptu appointment. Several minutes later, Dr. Ovie arrived and met with them in the parking lot. Dr. Ovie had been informed about the fever Hafeez is suspected to have had the previous day owing to his body temperature and lack of appetite. All covid-19 protocols were observed in full.

Dr. Ovie: "Wake Salau up."

Korede: "Okay doctor."

Dr. Ovie: "Good morning my friend, how are you?" Salau looks at his daddy and says,

"I'm not sick, I don't want an injection."

Dr. Ovie: "No I'm not giving you an injection. Daddy said you're now a big boy that you got up very early and dressed yourself and your brother for school." Salau smiles and doesn't say anything else. Dr. Ovie sanitizes his hands and raises Salau's eyelids and looks closely into his eyes and his tongue too.

"He's fine." The doctor said to his parents.

Dr. Ovie: "Wake Hafeez up." There was a great effort implored in getting Hafeez to wake up as he was fast asleep.

Dr. Ovie: "Hello Hafeez. How are you?" Hafeez is gripped by fear, squeezing his mother, he would not answer. "I'm not giving you an injection." Dr. Ovie added. "See my pocket, no injection." He concluded.

Hafeez: "Lemme see that other pocket." Everyone burst into laughter.

Dr. Ovie: "See, it's a pen that's in there, not a needle."

Hafeez: "Okay, so can you tell my mummy and my daddy to take me to school, there's a lot of work to do in school." His parents and Salau are staring at him.

Dr. Ovie: "What work are you going to do in school?"

Hafeez: "My new friend said I should tell my all classmates about Queen mother Idia "

Dr. Ovie: "Queen who?"

Olamilekan: "Which new friend?"

Korede: "Queen who?"

Hafeez: "Queen mother Idia, that's who he said I should tell my friends in school about. My friend, he's always standing by the window, he comes when he has something to tell me to do. But there are plenty of them, I hear their voices."

Dr. Ovie: "Did he help you get dressed today?"

Hafeez: "Yes, all of them helped us!"

Korede: "*Mogbe*! All of them? Blood of Jesus! No weapon formed against me and my family shall prosper..." She starts praying loudly, drawing the attention of other people around the parking lot.

Olamilekan: "Ovie, there was nobody else in the house, no one else entered my house this morning. However, I remember when I carried him to sleep this morning the window was open in the living room and also when I went to get Salau ready for school at six am or so, the window was open. So I don't know what to say."

Dr. Ovie, taking Olamilekan to a corner said, "When children this young talk so convincingly like they are, I believe them. I might not have to basically or logically agree with them but I do agree he has a friend and that there's a task he's been given. Help him with it. Take him to school and make sure he carries on the instructions from his fairytale friend. In time you'll meet with this friend of his."

"Ovie you de mad. Make me carry my pikin wey see demons go school. See make I tell you, from here na church straight. This one no be fever, na spiritual attack and na better holy water go cool every demon down." Olamilekan said, feeling confused.

Dr. Ovie: "I no de against church or deliverance, but did you listen to your son? He has a friend. He wants to carry on with this friend's request. I suggest you follow this boy on this adventure to know this queen and understand whatever it is they want from young children."

Olamilekan: "Thank you Ovie. Make me and the mother tok, make we know wetin we go do next."

Dr. Ovie: "No wahala my guy. Take it calmly."

Olamilekan: "Yes boss."

They drove from the hospital to the school which is also in Ikeja. They reported that their sons were not feeling well and had taken them to the hospital. They maintained they needed them to stay home under observation until they were certain the boys were in top condition to return to school. The school authorities agreed to their request and urged them to do a covid-19 test before returning them to school in order not to put other students at risk. Olamilekan then drove his family to a church and all four of them alighted from the car. After having their body's temperature checked at the entrance gate of the cathedral church and wearing their face-masks properly they went in and requested a meeting with a pastor. There was counseling from the man of God and he advised the parents to pay more attention to what their children do; as little as just paying close attention to detail, you'll learn all there is to know about them.

4:50 pm

They got home then Korede, assisted by Kate, made food for the whole household and they all ate on the rectangular eight seat dining table.

Olamilekan: "Salau, come here."

Salau: "Daddy, I'm not hungry."

Olamilekan: "Hafeez, come here."

Hafeez: "Daddy, I'm not hungry." One by one all of the householders, save for Usman, were together having a meal.

Olamilekan and Korede had agreed to draw the boys closer in order to understand who his mysterious friend is, the queen woman Hafeez mentioned. They decided to split up and connect with the boys separately. The shock of witnessing them already dressed so early in the morning was cause for concern. They feared their sons were being tormented by dark spirits and might lose their minds. Then after the meal, the parents set out on a plan.

Olamilekan: "Salau, put off the TV"

Salau: "Please daddy, lemme play a little while longer. I'll turn it off, I promise."

Olamilekan: "Turn it off now, let's talk first."

Salau: "About what daddy?" still holding on to the controller, playing a motorbike racing game. "My food will still digest even as I play." He added.

Olamilekan: "Tell me son, what happened today?" Salau drops the controller and looks at his father and goes, "Will you believe what I'll tell you?" "Yes son, I'll believe everything you tell me." Olamilekan responded.

Salau: "Daddy, Hafeez and I have a little man friend called Kadrert and he comes to us on Sundays and on Wednesdays. Or sometimes when he's free. He says of himself that he is the god of memories, the keeper of time. He's an ascended ancestor..."

Olamilekan: "Hmmm!"

Salau: "He wants Hafeez and me to join him in his kingdom where he's lived for hundreds of years, keeping memories for all and only relevant thoughts, words and actions."

Olamilekan: "Why did you say he's little?" Salau burst into laughter, "Daddy his leg doesn't touch the ground, so even though

20

he's floating we know he's short. Hafeez calls him a short man. He covers his face also." Salau replied.

Olamilekan: "Where can we meet him?, if we want to pay him a visit."

Salau: "Daddy he's here, now and always. All you have to do is to call him. He has a name he said we should call him on when we meet with our friends in school."

Olamilekan: "What name son?"

Salau: "It's Hafeez that can remember, he's really close friends with Hafeez. They laugh together all the time."

Olamilekan: "Is he a nice guy?"

Salau: "Of course, he's really nice, daddy he told Hafeez he was going to get a PS4 for him and then you brought it home and rightly, you said it was for Hafeez."

Olamilekan: "Hafeez asked a spirit being for PS4? I'm smacking that boy..."

"No daddy, Hafeez asked you first, you refused. Then he asked his friend and he assured him he'll get it for him. He only pleaded that we took our homework seriously; that members of the black-race are assiduous." Salau added.

Olamilekan: "Okay! Assiduous."

Korede: "My baby, what's going on?"

Hafeez: "Nothing is going on mom. I assure you everything is fine."

Korede: "Okay love, if you say so. What's this dream you're having?"

Hafeez: "Mom please calm down, there's nothing to worry about. I have a friend who comes to me in my dream but he's real, he said he's the keeper of memory and a slave to the queen. He said he wants me to help him remind my classmates of a people; the black person, to tell of our heritage, our ancestry and the life we lived before the European invasion of our beloved home, Africa."

Korede: "A real friend that comes to see you in your dream? Baby real people come to us physically and tell us where to join them, not in dreams."

Hafeez: "Mom chill."

Korede: "Oh! So, is all this about politics? Why does he want you to know about all that African stuff? Is he trying to do political things with my baby? doesn't he or them understand you're just a kid?"

Hafeez: "He said kids are the best to relive and convey the memories of old when it's planted in them. Our incorruptible nature makes us perfect vessels to carry on with the dreams and aspirations, the rich tradition of ancient Africa our fore parents enjoyed before the destructive and looting white people came."

Korede: "Hmmm! What should I do? Baby is he the one that makes you now talk like an adult? That makes you have grown man sense at your age; why is he teaching you all these complex stuff at your tender age?"

Hafeez: "C'mon mom, you know I'm a bright child." Chuckles, arms folded and legs crossed, sitting on the kitchen counter where his mother placed him.

Korede: "I don't really know how to respond to you. I just hope these demons haven't taken over you completely, that I'll be talking and they'll be responding inside you, before they'll go and know our plans to save you. I only used to watch on TV evil possessed people talk back at preachers, I didn't think my infant would tell me to calm down. I wish for you to talk to me like my child, like my baby boy. I don't know what has gotten into you. You're too mature for a baby."

Hafeez: "Stop crying mom, I'm fine." Korede is devastated, she says, "Twenty-four hours ago you called me mummy, now I'm mom. Where did my baby go? Someone please bring my baby boy back to me and flee with this old person in my baby's clothes." she cried louder.

Olamilekan and his wife had jointly phoned and informed their superiors at their places of work that they'd be taking the day off to attend to their ill children. There weren't any objections to their requests as the times and seasons didn't allow for taking chances. Korede's boss gave her till Monday to resume, however, he told her to run a test for the virus before returning to work for the safety of the rest of the staff. Their children could have contacted the virus as children also could be carriers.

Olamilekan and Korede meet up in the kitchen and the boys are playing motorbike racing in the living room.
Korede: "What do we do?"
Olamilekan: "I don't know. I'm confused. They're too young to take them seriously, minors live in this fantasyland where they connect with all kinds of fairytale stories and live in them; however, in this case, the windows are always open and both their stories are coherent. They were both dressed up for school, which scares me the most."
Korede: "We have to find a way to stop them; whatever they are. We must get these demons out of their heads."

"Hafeez, what is the name of the queen?" Olamilekan said,
"Queen mother Idia!" He responded from the living room.
Olamilekan: "Let's google search for it."
Korede: "Okay. Salau where's my phone? Salau!"
"I didn't take it." He responds,
Korede: "If I come and meet you there playing that game, c'mon will you go and get my phone from where you dropped it. When I was cooking I saw you with it. Because you'll never let go of my phone." Salau paused the game and dropped the controller.
"Don't press play." Salau said to Hafeez and he ran upstairs in search of his mothers phone.

They clicked searches for Queen Mother Idia and found images and art-works of a woman who lived in the sixteenth century and mother of the seventeenth Oba of the Benin kingdom in present day Nigeria. This marveled Olamilekan who has had interest in ancient African history. They read extensively about the kingdom, the Obas and the successions, the tradition, the role of women, the wars, the security forces, the conquests, their architecture and engineering, their interactions with the white people, their subsequent destruction and the looting of their wares by the Europeans. They studied historical accounts of different historians and came across treaties signed by African leaders erroneously ceding power and control over their territories to the

Europeans who then destroyed their structures, looted artifacts and distorted their heritage.

"From what their fellow Oyibos are saying that I'm reading, these Oyibo people are thieves o. They came and packed everything to their countries, and are using them to collect monies from tourists and they are not remitting the same funds to the countries they stole from. Okay, I believe in those days stealing was allowed as the queens and kings and the governments of that era sent voyages to Africa to steal and bring back home for national partake; they still stole our people to work their farms and cities too; but what about now? Equity and fairness is now widely known and embraced. Why are they still holding back monies they get from securing our artifacts from us? *Oboi!*" Olamilekan said out loud.

"Are you asking me?" Korede said,

"No, I'm just saying o! Because the funds they collect will be running into millions of dollars. As in, seeing some of these photos is truly disturbing. Worst is they changed the narrative, leaving modern Africans to think they have no history, no heritage, no records of greatness. They paint a faint and doom picture of Africa, they depict blacks as secondary beings whereas they are second class humans to blacks, their kings and queens permitted large scale criminality in Africa hundreds of years ago. They came with guns and killed, maimed, and looted the mineral resources to build their cities in Europe. They change the narrative and misinform their children to look down on a continent that gave their great-grandparents food and hope. From what I see written here, the Benin kingdom was finer and more productive than London before the British arrived. Then they destroyed the cities, burned down hundreds of years of civilization." Olamilekan said. His mood changed. Korede was quiet.

"What could be the reason that this friend of theirs wants them to know these things from the past? It's in the past, is it not, what's the use for all this information today?" Olamilekan was pondering,

"I'm not sure, perhaps it is to awaken the minds of modern Africans to the strength that lie underneath their black skin. Especially African women and girls. Maybe it's to show the black woman that there have lived great queens before them and they ought to pride themselves on being Africans instead of trying to look like Barbie dolls, they want long hair- bone-straight. Pathetic! Nails fixed, eyebrows fixed, hair fixed. We don't even have confidence in ourselves without modification. This is our personal reminder that we are not lower class and we could remain natural and still glow and shine." Korede said.

Olamilekan: "You, how many do you have?"

Korede: "How many what?"

Olamilekan: "Bone-straight hair stuff."

Korede: "We're not talking about me."

Olamilekan: "That thing is evil, I'm not buying it again."

Korede: "You will buy! Lemme just tell you, that my second one, that eighteen inches one, your younger sister said she's coming to take it. I told her no, that I'll bring it to her. If she comes here and I don't make up my mind, she'll carry more than one; that your sister has a sweet mouth. Don't forget she supported me to marry you, so I owe her. My point is you'll replace the one she's taking. Or rather the ones she's taking; so you'll just replace them, and don't buy again. Well, then if you want the mother of your children to be looking rough and dirty, that's okay."

Olamilekan: "How much is the hair, the bone-straight my sister is taking? Let me see if I can just buy her new ones."

Korede: "Everything is four-fifty!"

Olamilekan: "Mscheeeeeew!"

Korede: "No baby, it's because it's my girl I'm getting it from, else it's six hundred."

Olamilekan: "A whopping house rent money for another person's hair."

The couple joined their sons in the living room and made them sit on the floor, forming a circle. Korede started with teaching some bit of African history and Nigerian history. They were excited and Hafeez claimed his friend will be happy when he hears they're learning about queen mother Idia.

After dinner, they continue to teach them about more African history. They taught them about King Mansa Musa, the tenth Mansa of the Mali empire of the fourteenth century. Unarguably one of the richest men in world history. Also about Sunni Ali Ber, the first king of the Songhai empire. The boys were particularly happy when Korede was reading out to them and Olamilekan was showing them illustrations to help visualize the stories. They decided to take them history classes every Wednesday and Sunday as Salau claims the friend comes on Sundays and Wednesdays. For a moment Salau and Hafeez didn't bother about video games. They paid attention to the stories been told to them. They listened to their parents and asked questions about what they were taught. Kate isn't left out of the tutorials, even though visibly uninterested, they call her to join them from the dining table where she's sitting, they appoint her leader of the home-lesson believing that what's good for the goose is good for the gander.

Korede: "Back then, Africans didn't bother about Europe or even visiting there, they stayed home and developed their territories. Building and expanding as their knowledge and as their ability allowed them. Managing their resources and being content. Then Europe came in ships and vessels with lies, ammunition and ill-intent. They told us our gods are weak and introduced to us religiosity and adherence, which turned us to always make use of help, always requesting, instead of using our heads and hands. They then told us our names aren't presentable and wouldn't fetch us prosperity, and called us names that further damaged our personalities and made us question our place in the scheme of things. They later said our land is cursed and isn't good enough and that our color didn't fit mankind. Forced the few they could steal into boats and ferried them to work their farms, economies and cities- as unfit for mankind as we were. Now, after completing the task of fighting their wars, gaining for them an identity, building their cities and economies, they insist we're still beneath.

Sadly, we on our part have lost touch with ourselves that we choose the West over our ancestral lands and claim to be equal where we aren't. We have forgotten the us that we were before

the criminals, murderers and manipulators came. Kate, especially you, know this and know peace, that the black-race is the superior race. We must stop giving up our cultural values for those of the West."
Olamilekan "Black Beatles!" He laughs.

11:50 pm
Kate was first to leave the living room to her room upstairs after Korede denied her request to do the dishes that night, then followed by Korede herself. Olamilekan slept off on the couch watching the boys play a game. He didn't want them out of his sight. They were playing a football game. Only Salau played most of the time. Hafeez is indeed young to understand the complexity of the controllers. And he's quick to cry when Salau scores his team. Hafeez is an Anioma FC supporter just like his father, whereas Korede and Salau support Eko United FC.

Thursday 9 April, 2020
3:00 am
Olamilekan wakes up on the couch. The television set is on. The windows are open letting high current breeze in, blowing up the pages of the history materials on the center table. The air conditioner is on. Salau and Hafeez are sleeping on the Persian rug in the middle of the living room, both of them separated by the center table. All the reading materials are scattered everywhere on the marble floor with the pages wide open as if they have been read.

Chapter four.
NEWLAND high school, Agege, Lagos
GAMES FESTIVAL

1:33 pm

Tinuke Ajose, elder sister to Salau and Hafeez, is a sixteen year old football player and captain of her team. She's in SS3, her final year in secondary school and was determined to make it to the National games representing her school, NEWLAND High school. She desires football.

The National games festival is a complete sports festival organized by the federal government, implemented by the federal ministry of youths and sports development. The National games festival is broadly divided into two, Academic and Athletics. Under the Athletic category, there are two main divisions, School Athletics and Community Athletics. There were three main ways to get qualified and selected for the National games; by beating a set time-limit for mostly track and field events, by winning the school's top position for that particular sport and by recommendation from a state or local government office. Athletes who didn't belong to any school but were eligible to participate in the games representing their states, were mostly drawn through the first category- beating a particular set time-limit for the sporting event under the Community Athletics program.
The festival is preceded by pre-qualification competitions that are organized with elimination rounds which serve as auditions for qualifying to the games. This year's event is special because in the previous year, the games didn't take place due to the lockdown occasioned by the pandemic to prevent the further spread of the virus. This year's version is nicknamed 'lockdown edition' and it has drawn a lot of private and corporate investors which invariably skyrocketed the prize money to be won by athletes in over fifty different sporting events. The mainstream media isn't taking the games for granted as companies have signed deals to broadcast all the games live in real time.

Tinuke is a boarding school student, the first-choice goalkeeper and captain of her team, the NEWLAND queens and doubles as the assistant captain of the entire school football community. It is barely four months until the opening ceremony of the games festival to be hosted by the Government of Edo state in southern

Nigeria and preparations are underway. There are two internationally recognized standard turfs within the school compound and three more that needed upgrade. The school football captain and his assistant had the weekly task to draw up roasters for the many track and field athletes for the usage and optimization of the sport facilities within the school. This task was daunting, so the captain and his assistant enlisted the help of class reps, hostel reps and volunteers to supply names and hostels of students who were genuinely interested in participating in sports activities. There was a training facility built solely for school students who were interested in sports.

Tinuke's friend Vera, was a close friend of Udoka Umahi, the school's football captain and captain of the male team, the NEWLAND kings. Vera and Udoka were students of the previous set, the class of 2019; however Vera failed in her academic work and was advised to repeat the class, whereas Udoka applied to return for another term in other to participate in the National games festival. He would not be participating in academic work as he had done so during his set. He believed he had a chance at representing Nigeria in the Olympics if he made it to the festival and performed exceptionally well for the school team, that he might also get a call up to the under-20 squad of the Nigerian junior National team, the Flying Eagles. Tinuke in company with her friend Vera paid a visit to Udoka in the male ward of the training camp, a purpose built sports dormitory, about seven minutes walk from the female ward of the training camp, which is about eighteen minutes from the school hostel facility. They were told that Udoka has returned from the juvenile justice department of the police, after he was taken to the station and has been cleared of charges relating to theft.
"Hi King! Welcome back." Vera said as they drew closer to him, they were really excited to see him, for they feared the worst would have happened to him while in detention."
Udoka: "Hey queens! Good to see you both. I was thinking about letting you know I'm out and back."
Tinuke: "What happened over there?"
Vera: "We were worried about you."

Udoka: "Thank you guys. They took me there, started asking me questions about temper and anger..."

Vera: "I don't understand, I thought they detained you on charges of phone theft."

Udoka: "Yeah! That's what I thought too. But they told my mom they investigated and found me innocent of the allegations against me. Their annoyance is that I threatened to beat up any security-man or school staff who tries to open my locker."

Tinuke: "Oh! So did he make-up the story of a missing phone in your camp?"

Udoka: "No, it's true a phone was stolen; it was stolen by Joan's boyfriend..."

Tinuke: "Laide?"

Vera: "Laide?"

Udoka: "Yes, he did."

Tinuke: "Oh my gosh. What's his fate?"

Udoka: "He's been expelled."

Vera: "Wow!"

Udoka: "It's crazy."

Tinuke: "It's sad."

Vera: "It's more disappointing."

"I've got sad news though." Udoka said as he was lacing his football boots.

"What is it?" Vera asked, fully gazed at him,

"I've been disqualified from participating in the qualifiers." Udoka added,

"No they didn't!" Tinuke said.

"Yes o! For starting a quarrel and for issuing threats." He concluded.

"I'm so sorry." Vera said, "But isn't there a way to appeal the disqualification knowing you were falsely accused of stealing?" She added.

"I don't know, when we arrived at school from the police station my mom pleaded with the principal to review the decision but he vehemently opposed it. He maintained I was rude, disrespectful and disobedient." Udoka said. Vera starts sobbing.

Tinuke: "Maybe we should stage a protest in the principal's office this evening."

Udoka: "No way, imagine if the protest gets out of line, they'll expel me straight up. My mom pleaded that they review the disqualification and the principal promised to look into it later on. I'll be prayerful and hope it's lifted. Meanwhile, we have to start preparing for the games. We have to begin by selecting two teams that'll face GSS Ikoli and submit their names to *coachie* for final team selection. The match is on Saturday." Tinuke inserts her left hand in her pocket and brings out two sheets and hands it over to Udoka who peruses the sheets.

"Great work, I like the selection for the queens team." Udoka said, "Please add Maryam Sa'ad and Benedicta Dimka's so it'll make it a total of 25 names." He added.

"Okay!" Tinuke noted.

"As for the kings team, substitute my name for Jerome's, there's a strong likelihood I won't make the team, at least until the disqualification is reviewed." Udoka said,

"No, I won't." Tinuke rebuked him. "You're the captain, the most experienced player in the male team. Without you, there's a great chance we won't make it to the National." she added.

"Yes she's right!" Vera adds her voice. She continues, "Don't you ever give up on something good you want for yourself. You could have been in the university now had you chosen to give up your dreams of playing professional football. This is your best chance, the National games are watched on TV by scouts from every continent on earth. Many girls I know got scholarships to study abroad because of their qualities in sport. Like you said, hold on to prayer and never lose hope. GSS Ikoli is a tough opponent. They usually field older students to participate in the games they play. Even in chess, they are always difficult to beat. This team needs you."

"Thanks guys," Udoka said feeling happier. "You guys know these things but the school management don't, or they simply don't want me to be part of the team because this isn't my original set." He added,

"Don't bother about them, a bunch of sadists who didn't make it during their youth now they've agreed to deprive and deny prospective young people the opportunity to achieve their dreams, bringing up unnecessary drama to distract us. I'm not removing your name from the list. I'll submit it like that." Tinuke assured him.

Udoka: "Thanks guys, your words are surely appreciated. Please call for the campers to come out for the evening training session. Today we'll do light training; one kilometer jogging round the tracks for both male and female, then we close up with aerobics class. That will be it for the day. Meet me in the field."
Vera: "Very light indeed."
Tinuke: "Ai Ai captain." And the ladies departed.

Chapter five.
Friday 10th April, 2020
Surulere, Lagos
TROUBLE

Fridays are usually half-days as primary and secondary schools close at twelve noon. Most of the students however, do not go home as they play and play until the generally designated hour for closing, two o'clock in the afternoon. Due to the pandemic, schools boards nationwide decided to operate in shifts so as to reduce the number of students together at a particular time of the day. Primary one - primary three students, as well as Junior secondary school students of form one - three resume at eight in the morning and close at twelve noon. Likewise primary four - primary six students and senior secondary school students of form four - six resume at twelve noon and close at four in the afternoon. This was the case in Nashua Memorial primary school, Surulere, where Emeka and his brother Ejike are studying. Primary five and primary one respectively. Aniete concerns herself mostly with taking Ejike out to join the school bus and collecting him back home. Emeka is old enough to walk to school and back home, also because she couldn't afford to pay the school bus service for both of them.

11:50 am
Emeka is walking to school clad in his school uniform with a lunchbox in his left hand and a schoolbag behind his back; putting on smart sandals. He's just a few meters from the school fence when three boys appeared from the corner. Oliseh, Okechukwu and Nonso are all familiar faces. Oliseh and Okechukwu are friends and are older than Emeka, both at twelve years of age. Nonso is Oliseh's kid brother who, just a week ago, had been bullied by Emeka for bullying his kid brother Ejike. It was time for revenge on Emeka. Emeka is breathing hard upon sighting them from a distance. He stops, retrieves his schoolbag from his back, opens it and tucks his lunchbox in it, then he places the school bag on the floor, by his side. He's panicking.
Oliseh: "Look who we found. Superman. I heard you beat up Nonso because he was joking with your brother. You made Nonso cry, well it's your turn to cry."
Okechukwu: "Yes! It's your turn to cry. One turn deserves another." Nonso stands aside while Oliseh and Okechukwu spread out to grab Emeka. There, by the school fence were sand heaps, broken tiles, and dried up cement remains used for construction and were left on the site. In a flash, Emeka packed sand in both of his hands and threw it at them aiming for their eyes. Both of them Oliseh and Okechukwu are hit by the debris

thrown at them, they screamed to the top of their voices while Emeka ran towards Nonso, knocking him down and dashed to the school gate where he met safety. Nonso starts crying. As soon as he got to the school's gate he reported the incident to the security men at the gate. He was in tears at this moment and breathing heavily which led a staff member, Aunty Marie, to take it up with the parents of Nonso and Oliseh; but first, she escorted him back to the scene to pick up his school bag which wasn't harmed.

4:00 pm

Aniete is home with her sons Emeka and Ejike. Her oldest son, Udoka, is in a boarding house.

There's a knock on the door and Emeka answers to see who's there.

"Is your mummy home?" A dark skinned man inquired.

"Yes, she is." Emeka responds and lets him into the living room.

"Lemme go and get her." He added. "Mummy! Mummy, someone is looking for you." Emeka called out to his mother. Aniete walks into the living room, tying a wrapper round her waist and a t-shirt.

"Yes, how may I help you?" She asked the man.

"Thank you. My name is Idris Iliyasu and I work with the child protection unit of the Lagos state ministry of women affairs and infant development."

Aniete: "Okay, how may I help you?"

Idris: "We have received multiple complaints about your inability to bring up your children properly..."

Aniete: "Excuse me. What nonsense do you allow out of your mouth? And by the way, who is, or who are the people sending in those complaints?"

Idris: "Our informants are always kept private unless a competent court of law demands for their identities. We have been investigating you and your family since the demise of your husband. We found that you have sold his landed property as well as his stake in several companies which has led you to change the schools your children attend. For instance, your eldest son we have on record has chosen to redo his final year in NEWLAND high as you're unable to afford university tuition for him. Your inability to cater for these children is leading them to be angry and aggressive..."

Aniete: "Fool, clap for yourself. Talking about anger and aggression, if the amebo people who gossip about my family and I were the least sincere, they'll tell you my boy was falsely accused of stealing. That's why he became angry and was provoked by provocation. They'd have also reported that the matter was resolved and they absolved him of wrongdoing. And If you must know, he opted to redo his SS3 because it is his dream to play for his country if he makes the team for the National games. Tuition for university? How much is tuition? Leave my house. I said, leave my house."

Idris: "Well said, what then do you have to say about your eight year old son who out of malice and Ill-will almost blinded the eyes of two young boys for no reason at all. What do you have to say about that before we take you in for questioning? As we have already secured a warrant for your arrest from a competent court of law for your mental evaluation. Analysis shows there has been a decline in your family's general affairs deduced by your inability to properly, adequately cater for them being minors."

Aniete: "I don't understand."

Idris: "Your son almost blinded two boys earlier today on their way to school, the motive to injure was clear."

Aniete: "You speak about a motive regarding an eight year old? That cannot be; I'm not even aware. Right now I'm the least bothered about what you just said. Leave my house."

Idris: "Exactly, you're disconnected from them and their affairs. The state government will take care of them in a home designed for minors who have no one to cater for them until we ascertain whether or not you're fit to cater properly and adequately to their needs as we perceive you may be on substances that alter your mind, hence the mental assessment or evaluation if you may."

Idris Iliyasu calls out to three female police officers in a van outside, showing them an arrest warrant for Aniete Umahi to undergo mental assessment in the psychiatric hospital, Yaba and instructs them to arrest her. The officers walk into the house and try to snatch Aniete. As they attempt to hold her she resists being taken away and there is a mild drama going on in her living room.

Emeka and Ejike scream the loudest. "Leave our mummy alone!"
"Leave our mummy alone." until the neighbors gather round. The
boys are crying, Aniete is crying. The police officers are bent on
enforcing the arrest warrant. There's cursing here and there.
Aniete has vehemently refused to follow them.
"Chukwubuike, where are you? Where are you? Come now and
save us from these attackers. They're fighting your children, and
they want to take away your wife. Come now and rescue us. Oh!
Chukwubuike, please come to our aid." Aniete was screaming and
wailing.

The neighbors seek to quell the near-violent attempt to arrest
Aniete.
In the end, after about three hours plus of unsuccessful attempts
at taking her away, the child protection unit withdrew from
arresting her and left. The tugging and dragging left some of her
furniture broken and others displaced. She's sitting on the floor
holding on to Emeka and Ejike and all three, in addition with a
few concerned neighbors, were all in tears.
As the neighbors depart one after another, Aniete and her sons
hold hands together and pray. Hoping this incident brings to an
end months of misery and misfortune.

Chapter six.
NEWLAND high school, Agege, Lagos.
ONENESS

8:50 pm
Udoka and Vera take a walk from the cafeteria in the girls hostel and she's accompanying him to the male training camp. They're both holding their face-masks not covering and protecting their noses and mouths.
Vera: "So what's the plan? Assuming they don't recall you for pre-qualifying rounds."
Udoka: "I really don't know. Everything happened fast. It was all good just a week ago."
Vera: "Don't get mad, I have something to tell you."
Udoka: "What's that?"
Vera: "Okay so Tinuke and I decided to tell her dad about you and he promised to speak with the principal. He'd love to talk with you on the issue but Tinuke thought it wasn't a good idea for

him to speak with you, she felt you might not want to talk with him or anyone else about it. Well, it's not such a bad idea to seek out help."

Udoka: "Oboi!" He exclaims, "You guys actually did that for my sake?" He added.

Vera: "Yes, also for the team. All the teammates are behind you. Shhhh! Lemme tell you a secret! Promise me no one will hear. At least not that Vera said." Udoka smiles and says, "I promise, I'll tell no one."

Vera: "Great! All the football team players, both the kings and queens have agreed to boycott the games, I mean all the games if the school authorities fail to recall you." Tear drops left Udoka's eyes, obeyed gravity, rolled down his cheek and fell to the ground. "

"You mean all of them are sticking out their necks and risking their chances of participating for my sake?" a broken and melting Udoka asked.

"Yes, we all are." Vera responded.

"Even Obed?" He asked,

"All of them. Obed, James, Malik." she responded.

"O my gosh! Malik too?" Udoka is genuinely excited, unbelievable to him.

Vera: "Tinuke suggested a boycott. Jasper seconded, then the rest of the athletes unanimously agreed."

Udoka: "You're kidding me."

Vera: "Yo cry cry guy! Don't take it personal, everyone wants to make it to the National games, and nobody definitely wants to go to the Nationals and lose or make a fool of themselves. There's no doubt you're a top player and the best cheerleader the NEWLAND kings have got when you're on the bench." Her soothing words found a place within him and brought a smile forth upon his face. This was about the same time his mother and brothers were praying.

Udoka: "I can't thank you guys enough. Where's my assistant *skippo?*"

Vera: "She went home. She said something about her kid brother having weird dreams and seeing visions of ghosts."

Udoka: "Seeing what? Ghosts? Abeg o!"

Vera: "I told her to call Mrs. Yvone when she gets home so we can talk."
Udoka: "Did her parents come for her?"
Vera: "They ordered a cab to come pick her up."
Udoka: "When is she returning?"
Vera: "Tomorrow or Sunday."
Udoka: "Okay. I can't wait to let her know how grateful I am for rallying the guys to stand by me. Means I still got a chance to make it to the National games. Thank God, I'm super grateful to God. Matter of fact, what God cannot do does not exist."
Vera: "Yeah right!"

Chapter seven.
Friday 10 April, 2020
Ikeja, Lagos.
ACCIDENT

Tinuke got home before noon. The traffic from Agege to Ikeja was bone-crushing, patience draining and weakening to say the least. She had to go home, Korede told her disturbing things about her favorite brother Hafeez. She arrived to a warm welcome from her family. Olamilekan wasn't home, Usman informed her so when he opened the gate. She entered and washed her hands thoroughly to elbow level and used a hand-sanitizer she got from her pocket. Korede was excited to see her, just like Kate. Salau was playing a game so his attention was split into pieces. Hafeez screamed, dashed and jumped on her. They went straight to playing together; Hafeez sits on her thighs, while she is tickling him and getting the infant in him to respond, which happened to the surprise of Korede.
"Where is my Sharwarma?" Hafeez said,

"Over there, open that paper bag." She replied, "Two for you and one for everyone else." She added. Hafeez is thrilled, he's running and making noise, he's handing one wrap of super-spicy snack to everyone. Everyone is merry-making save for Salau.

"Will you drop that game and eat your Sharwarma before it gets cold?" Korede said to Salau.

"It's okay mummy, I like it when it's cold." Salau replied.

Tinuke: "Mummy, where is daddy?"

Korede: "I don't know, call him to say you're home. That may get him to come back before midnight."

"Okay mummy." She responded. "When are you going back to school?" Korede inquired. Tomorrow or Sunday. I have a game next week and I'd really love to be very competitive going in for the match up. Serious preparations are underway." Tinuke replied.

"How are your friends and teachers? Especially Mrs. Yvone." Korede added,

"They're all great. We're all busy working out ways and techniques to make the National games. Every young boy and girl wants to go to the games. Mummy, prize money for the bronze medal is three million Naira, the silver medal is four million, while the gold medal is five million mummy, minus dash from state governors, as in! Okay that's for individual sporting events o, team events have even more money for the winners. Mummy I can get a life for myself, fund it by myself and be independent of you and daddy." Tinuke said, Korede responded saying,

"Wow! That's a whole lot of money for young people. That can go a long way in footing their tertiary education fees. Kudos to the government and the corporate sponsors."

Tinuke: "Hello daddy, I'm home. Yes daddy! I thought you'd be home when I get here. I'm waiting o. Not yet, no she hasn't. But I can perceive it. No, it's not ready yet. Okay daddy. I love you too."

Korede: "What was he saying?.

Tinuke: "That, why haven't you given me something to eat, that he didn't know I was visiting, he'd have emphasized that his firstborn-fruit is coming home before leaving the house."

Korede: "Don't mind him, he's never at home, always busy this busy that. Busy here and there."
Tinuke: "Don't mind daddy. Hafeez come here my baby."
Hafeez: "Tinuke, where are your gloves? I wanna be a goalie when I grow up."
Kate: "You want to be everything." Responding to Hafeez.
Tinuke: "I left the pair in camp, I'll get small ones for you..."
Hafeez: "I don't want small ones, I want big ones, I want it so when I'm big I'll be a goalkeeper for Nigeria."

Korede has been paying attention to Hafeez since Tinuke arrived. She's observing that he's returning to being a kid again, not responding like an adult to questions and occurrences.

After lunch, Tinuke takes time out with Salau. She's asking him questions about his affairs with the mystery friend of theirs. Salau repeated all he'd said to his parents and to the doctor. Tinuke then asked Salau to invite their friend to the house that evening because she wanted to meet with him, her being interested in traditional African history.
"Tinuke, just ask Hafeez to tell him to come over, he's closer to Hafeez than he is to me, I'm mostly there because Hafeez cannot be left all by himself so I join in." Salau said,
"Do you mean the older one is responsible for the younger ones when you guys meet?" Tinuke added,
"Yes." Salau replied.
Tinuke goes to her mother and informs her that she's willing to go on the adventure with Hafeez. That she was ready to trade in places with Salau for him to be set free.
Tinuke: "Mummy, I'm joining Hafeez to see the Queen mother. After speaking with Salau and Hafeez, I came to understand that the meeting will mainly focus on bringing the past occurrences into the present day for the benefit of today and the future. And we must agree that righting yesterday's wrong for the better, brighter tomorrow is key. We must all join hands to make it work."
Korede: "You must be out of your mind. You're not going anywhere. And don't let your father hear you say that. What do

you mean you want to go and meet with a woman that died more than five hundred years ago? Where is this place you'll meet her? Don't you think this is an attempt to journey to hell? Leave these children alone, they're overreacting to childhood. Stop thinking you're going anywhere with anybody. Am I making myself clear?"

Tinuke: "Mummy! Please chill, it doesn't seem scary and dark and negative as you're painting it. It's time travel, I've read a lot about these things, plus, my brother might be in possible danger which I can just be able to avoid. And all things being equal, we'll be back before you know it and most importantly, these people or things, whatever they are, will go away and stop disturbing my brothers. That way I can focus on football."

Korede: "You're out of your mind. Look I'm your mother, I can never mislead you, this my tummy is where I carried you for nine months, I can never lie to you. Please, you're not going anywhere, they too aren't going anywhere either. Remove this nonsense from your head, they're just watching too much cartoon and, well I said it, but he'll never listen. That video game is the enemy; ever since that game came into my house my boys changed. Salau doesn't do anything if it can't be done near the TV set, Hafeez got a friend after that game came. If I talk, your father will say I'm superstitious. Now my daughter wants to go and see a queen. Jesus please! I've started my nine days novena to confuse and scatter them anywhere they're meeting, thinking of, or even mentioning the names of my family members. Anywhere the pictures of my children are, I blind them in Jesus name!"

Tinuke: "Mummy I've told you o! Don't say I didn't tell you."

4:40 pm

Olamilekan returns home with a guest, professor Rowland Akeredolu. Olamilekan was advised to seek the counsel of Professor Akeredolu, a physicist, philosopher and historian. He drove all day to meet with and collect him from his Ikorodu residence. Professor Akeredolu was on his way out of Lagos when he agreed to make a detour to the Ajoses.

Mr. Akeredolu wore a grey suit, with matching brown belt and shoes. He has a hat on. Olamilekan shows him to the dining table upon which he drops a black suitcase he walked in with, from which he brings out Palm leaves bound together by a tiny black thread and holds it in his mouth. He pulls and takes a seat. From the suitcase he brings out about four sheets of paper bound together with tiny black threads at the extreme left and begins to read out enchanting words audibly. He was speaking in Atori. Sitting at the dinner, he calls Salau to sit with him. Minutes later he called Hafeez also. Olamilekan, Korede, Tinuke and Kate were all in the living room watching the scenes unfolding from that distance. Meanwhile, Tinuke is super happy to meet her daddy. Korede isn't particularly happy Olamilekan got a man who practiced faith contrary to the Christian doctrines, however she kept mute and looked on. When she couldn't take it anymore, she queried him whispering,
"Who is this man you brought here, I hope he's not going to worsen the situation the kids are in?" "No babe, this one is trained to communicate with the worlds beyond. It's not everybody that has the calling for extraterrestrial stuff. All he's here for is to tell us exactly what these children are trying to say, especially about the queen mother and a visit to meet with her. Just all that stuff. It's necessary to see farther than the pastors can go; there's levels to the vision thing. It's the same thing babe, the betterment of our children; I'm their father, I'm responsible." Olamilekan replied.

Mr. Akeredolu spoke with the boys for not more than five minutes each. He's taking down notes on the reverse side of the sheets of paper bound together. After some quiet time, he calls Olamilekan and Korede to join him at the dinner.
Holding the palm leaves in his hand he says, "Dear friends, I am pleased to inform you that starting with your household, a new wave of consciousness has awoken. The spirits of your ancestors, spirits of our ancestors want us to thread a new path, one which will entail searching for ourselves and finding us within us for the betterment of our kind. This consciousness is driven by the infants, the young people you see who have no corruption in their hearts to deliver the black race free from imperialism without

44

violence and destruction. But with dialogue assisted by spirits of our ancestors, also by correcting historical accounts to align with the true narrative. This suggests a trip back five hundred years ago." He confirmed all the boys had been saying long ago about the presence of a mysterious friend and an invitation to meet with the queen mother Idia. Akeredolu stressed that the meeting with the queen mother and other members of the Iyoba cabinet was to officially establish an awareness of the black heritage before savagery arrived on boats and ships.

"The reason for Hafeez and Salau wanting to meet with their classmates was to raise a unified consciousness amongst them and to further spread the message of liberation from the shackles of modern slave-masters. It is the will of our ancestors that this time and season present itself and that we, modern blacks, take up the challenge and spread the words of freedom to the ends of Africa and beyond." Professor Akeredolu concluded.

Olamilekan: "We don't understand."

Akeredolu: "Your son Hafeez has been handpicked by a legion of ancestors to play two roles, one in our time, which he has already begun and another in ancient times. I see clearly that the spirits of our fathers long gone are interested in sending Hafeez farther back in time to warn a certain man, Musa Mansa, abi is it Mansa Musa, the ruler of the Mali empire not to go on a journey with such tremendous amount of precious metals, as that drew the attention of the world to the wealth of Africa which kicked off the start of white attraction to Africa and the subsequent scramble and partition of the continent."

Korede: "I don't get it! My Hafeez is going where?"

Olamilekan: "We read about Musa Mansa a while ago to them, there was no part of allowing him to visit anyone for whatever reason."

Korede: "Let the ancestors go there themselves. I won't allow a baby to go on such an impossible task in his dream. What if something happens, how do I get my boy back? How do I watch over him, or I should just sit by his bedside and fan him?"

Akeredolu: "That's exactly why the spirits of our ancestors have enlisted his favorite sibling, Tinuke to join him..."

Korede: "Don't even talk my daughter into this, she had no business being in this mix. I only informed her of what was going on while she's away."

Akeredolu: "Madam, everything that happens in life has been decided in the spirit. This is just a mere manifestation of the decisions reached in the life that precedes this life. Like that video game they're playing was decided already in spirit before the task of its physical manifestation was thrown on your shoulder. Same as the choice of guardian, caretaker or harbinger of the messenger has been chosen."

Tinuke: "But how can this be, I have fixed games to partake in school. How do I abandon all that commitment and accompany Hafeez into the past, what If I never return?"

Akeredolu: "Nature will ferry you to where you must be. In the fullness of time, all things will fall perfectly in place."

Professor Rowland Akeredolu departed from the residence of the Ajoses'.

Olamilekan walks briskly in front of the guest, opens the exit door and stands by it. Korede accosts the guest and says, "Daddy please tell me my boys are alright. I don't know what's going on."

"I can't tell, I'm mortal in full. What I said is all I saw. Pay attention to their details." Akeredolu replied.

Next was Tinuke. She walked out of the house and stood closely with professor Akeredolu.

Tinuke: "I feel a need to be by his side. I can coordinate him better than Salau."

Akeredolu: "Be by his side then."

Tinuke: "How do I know what and where?"

Akeredolu: "What and where, when and how will reveal itself."

She withdraws to the house and hold her mother, while professor Akeredolu joins Olamilekan in the car. Usman opens the gate and Olamilekan reverses out of the compound.

8:20 pm

Hafeez plays a prank on Tinuke, he covers himself with a white bedsheet and hides himself behind the door to his and Salau's room. He then calls out to Tinuke several times. Tinuke walks towards the sound of his voice and to the room in search of him.

Hafeez sneaks up behind her and scares the hell out of her, then dashes out of the room laughing. Frightened and embarrassed, Tinuke chases after Hafeez. Amidst the plethora of objects on the floor of the boys room consisted of building blocks, clothes, shoes, flip flops, toys. Tinuke steps on a toy firefighter-van on the floor which rolls and she twists her left ankle; in motion she flips and smashes her left elbow on the door of the room and she lands on the floor. Hafeez walks back to her, his smile turned up-side-down, staring at her lying helplessly on the floor, moving slowly in pain and anguish, his heart skipping beats and he starts crying. "Mummy! Mummy! Mummy!" He's yelling. Kate rushes out of a bathroom upstairs and on seeing Tinuke lie on the floor, joins in the chorus of screaming "Mummy!" multiple times.

9:14 pm
Korede, being an aide worker, was calm on the surface owing to several training on mind and situation control she's undergone over the years. She carefully lifts Tinuke up, but for fear she might have fractured a part of her body, opts for help from Usman. Kate hurriedly gets Usman who carries Tinuke on his shoulder downstairs into Korede's waiting SUV. Kate phones Olamilekan and informs him Korede is taking Tinuke to the hospital. There's panicking everywhere. Usman drove in the car with Korede; Tinuke was on his lap. She's groaning. There's no traffic on the way to the hospital, and eventually the trio arrived at Tagoon hospital, Ikeja.
Securityman: "Good evening Ma."
Korede: "Open up please! It's an emergency. Please sir."
Securityman: "I'm sorry Ma, but we have to conduct a body temperature check before you can go in, also you have to wear your nose-masks."
Korede: "My baby is dying, please I need to get her to ICU."
Securityman: "I'm sorry Ma, this is standard practice since the outbreak of the virus. I'm sorry my job is on the line disobeying orders."
Usman: "Oga abeg no vex, we forget to carry face-mask commot from house. Na Rush we rush wen we hear children de shout. Abeg help us make this girl no die. Abeg no vex. Okay where we

47

go buy face-masks, night don do?" Usman persuaded the security officials to consider their situation and assist a helpless child. Korede was helpless, she kept pressing the horn. Reluctantly, the gate was opened and Korede drove in straight to the ICU where Tinuke was lifted carefully by hospital staff and placed on the stretcher. Korede explained to a nurse who asked the nature of the accident, that Tinuke tripped and fell and may have landed on her neck, or may have fractured her neck. She was made to sit down. Olamilekan was told at the ICU when he arrived that his daughter had been moved to the theater. He got to the theater and met with Korede.

"You see what you caused? You brought the devil into our home, see now what has become of us and our children." Korede attacks Olamilekan. "Put yourself together, woman. I told you in the first place not to invite Tinuke home, you refused; see what her presence has caused. The poor girl has qualifying matches to play over the weekend." Olamilekan responded.

"I didn't ask her to come over. I told her what was happening in the house so she could be more prayerful. Don't blame me for her insisting on seeing Hafeez. Besides If you hadn't bought that video game all these wouldn't have happened; none of these would have started." Korede added,

"PlayStation has never hurt anybody. Professor Akeredolu and my father are friends. I discussed with my father about the fate of his grandson and he contacted Prof. Luckily prof. was just on his way back to his base in Kogi state. I picked him from Ikorodu and took him to the airport as soon as we left the house. That's why I wasted time. We spoke until the final boarding announcement. He's from Ekiti state but has settled in Ankpa, in Kogi state. He's a master in metaphysical matters and a visiting professor at the university of Kogi's school of wizardry-advanced. He's not a bad person." Olamilekan responded.

Olamilekan: "But wait, why are you always quick to apportion blame on me for everything. No matter what happens, you'll blame me. In your sight I'm always wrong for everything I do. You're available only to blame me. Watching my parents, I thought a man and his wife are a team fighting for their own collective good. But I don't feel that support from you. Every time, I fear I'm going to be attacked and just like I think, you go on and attack me." Korede stayed muted.

Olamilekan: "You must talk. What did I ever do to you? You've repeatedly said I'm not your preferred man, you've told everyone. Fine, I didn't get upset. But when you see your first daughter going seventeen why not just take everything as the will of God? Do you still feel sad over marrying someone seventeen-plus years later? I'm sick and tired of your constant blame-game. I bought a car, issue. I bought a massive flatscreen, issue. I moved to the duplex, issue. What do you want from me anyway? Look woman, I don't want anymore of your incessant nagging and fights..." Dr. Ovie enters the waiting room in front of theater 4.

Dr. Ovie: "Guy wetin you de quarrel over this night? Cool down, night don do."

Olamilekan: "Thank God, Ovie, I'm really happy to see you. Dem de inside with my girl. Just enter make yu see wetin dem de do."

Dr. Ovie: "No issue. Stop to de fight your woman." He's wearing his lab-coat and gloves to join in the theater room.

"I no de fight anybody." Olamilekan said. Korede was crying when Dr. Ovie's wife came and covered her with a jacket. Dr. Ovie's wife joined him in the hospital after getting a call from Olamilekan that his daughter had been hospitalized; it was late at night, almost twelve midnight.

After forty-eight minutes, Dr. Ovie walks out of the theater with a doctor on-call holding x-ray sheets and intimating that Tinuke fell and fractured her collarbone and her right wrist shifted. It would keep her out of sporting events for maybe three to four months. He assured Korede that she would be fine.

Dr. Ovie led them, Korede and Olamilekan, and they walked into the theater to see Tinuke on life support. But her face is ever radiant, emitting hope amidst doubt. Korede in company with Kasarachi Ovie and Usman return home for some rest and to watch over the boys and Kate.

Dr. Ovie: "Wetin happen?"

Olamilekan: "Na phone dem call me say Tinuke fall. I say which kind of fall goalkeeper never fall wey be say na hospital tins. My brother, I just tire. This matter wan make me vex o."

Dr. Ovie: "Who yur wife say you carry home? E get wetin she de whisper to my wife."

Olamilekan: "Professor Akeredolu. Okay wetin happen be say, as we leave you, we go church, normal. Dem pray finish, tok everything. We reach house, we begin to read the history of African kings, queens and famous people of African origin to di boys. Normal stuff. Korede say she wan tell Tinuke, I say no need, say di girl get competition wey she de prepare for, say make we no distract her. Before I know wetin de happen, Tinuke de house. Well, dat one no be issue. I tok wit my pops about my boys, popci say make I consult im guy Ake. Na im nickname be dat, Ake. E gimme number make I call di man say di man de see outside tins. Say na di man see all dia exams scores dat year for university. E tell di ones wey go fail say dem go fail. This Ake man tell everyone of dia set mates how dem go do collect scholarship study abroad, which happened. So dem get massive respect for dia guy. Na im I go track professor for Ikorodu carry am come house."

Dr. Ovie: "So wetin professor tok."

Olamilekan: "My man, prof. tok many tins o. Prof. say na legit o. Say di Benin woman don choose my boy wit many oda children to time-travel, to go clear one chairman like dat say make e no cast many many shine-shine stones on im journey to Mecca dat year, say e go cast us and say our army neva solid to match dia own army for war."

Dr. Ovie: "I no understand."

Olamilekan: "Doc, no be small tok o. No be wetin we go stand tok, na sidon sumtin. Say na my boy di gods choose to to deliver di message. I no even know weda to believe or not. Wen we de go airport, prof. say all those artifacts wey Oyibo steal, say dem still de alive o. Say the spirits wey commission those artifacts de connect with the queen mother crown. Oyibo steal them because dem no know wetin de behind the creation. Dem carry religion come use as excuse scatter our heritage, now we no get identity, we no get yesterday. Little wonder all man de migrate. We no sabi ourselves anymore because we de use Oyibo man eyes take see road for our country. So wetin Oyibo say e good, we agree say e good. Wetin Oyibo say e bad, we agree say e bad. Foreign names

we de bear, foreign gods we de serve. Professor yarn many tins o.
E say queen mother spirit no gree rest, say her, along wit spirits of
many more great kings and queens of time-past come present time
to prepare young Africans for the task in adulthood, the task of
awakening a consciousness of the lives and times of the black-race
before the era of slave-trade and repatriation of the lost treasures
of Africans from the white looters back home. Just imagine, na im
dis one come de happen wit my Tinuke now. My brother I weak."
Dr. Ovie: "Oboi! E be tins!"

Chapter eight.
Saturday 11 April, 2020
NEWLAND high school, Agege, Lagos.
GAME TIME

3:00 pm

"You know you don't have to teach someone something for them to learn, especially children. Those your silent acts and omissions are those you repeat often, translates to the ones people see and encounter often, that's the one they'll imitate, master and emulate, especially children. There's learning by sight."

"For whatever reason why you said that, I agree. Well, yes of course, all the skills we'll use to scatter your defense, humiliate you guys and embarrass your goalie this afternoon, we learned them on TV. We search for the moves we want on set-pieces and practice them."

"Impressive, same as the dance steps we'll celebrate with after each goal we score you kids in front of your principal, we also learned in music videos. Took a long time for the whole team to practice and perfect the ones you'll be seeing this afternoon."

"I agree with you, there's learning by sight only."

"May the best team win!"

"May the best team win!"

Both captains of NEWLAND high kings and GSS Ikoli tease each and exchange pleasantries, while grouping for pre-match photo. The stands are empty; yes, due to the pandemic. The fixture began a series of matches for qualifying for the National games festival. The top three overall secondary schools from each state of the federation qualify automatically. This is obtained by adding up general statistics and all data available for all the games played; minutes with ball-possession, total goals scored, total goals conceded, total assists, fouls committed and with a range of other information compiled by the football federation. There's playoffs for the schools that qualified lower.

The fixture for the NEWLAND Queens in the football category for this round of qualification is with St. Bridget's girls secondary school, the defending champions in that football category slated for next week Saturday.

The starting lineup and the substitute bench list were void of Udoka Umahi. The lineup was secret until two o'clock in the afternoon; general tactics training was done with all present at training. Regardless, he trained with the rest of the boys minutes before kickoff and could compete to be the cheerleader of the match standing on the sidelines. GSS Ikoli scored first in the fifteenth minute of the first-half after the ball was square-played into the eighteen yard box from the far right and easily tapped between the legs of the NEWLAND high school goalkeeper, Obed. The game became more interesting and tense when a NEWLAND high school student, Nansel Ejim was red carded for an awful tackle in the eighteenth minute. The rest of the firsthalf didn't produce any more goals. The second half saw two changes by the NEWLAND high school management team and one change by Ikoli boys. The battle for the midfield went on throughout the second half with the one-man advantage taking a toll on the home team.

Then came an equalizer. NEWLAND high responded, Jasper scored a wonder goal with a header for his first goal of the qualifying round of games. Then the Ikoli boys added a second when the host defenders failed to clear the ball from the penalty box-area for two goals to one. Then later on, there was an equalizer by Jasper a few minutes later for his brace. There was hope on the bench after Jasper scored the second goal, there was real hope. The home players were all out to get maximum points. As the game heated up and at ten minutes to stoppage time, Ikoli boys capitalized on a loose ball and slotted home the ball in the back of the net from close range. GSS Ikoli came out with a convincing 3:2 win over their hosts, NEWLAND high school. This means NEWLAND high kings must win their last two games to qualify from the group stages. The loss to GSS Ikoli was a hard pill to swallow, it was demoralizing and it was further emphasized when the principal of the school read the riot act to the athletes and informed them of the consequence of boycotting the competition because of punishment meted out on Udoka which he believed was the reason they lost. The principal argued they didn't play to their full capacity. In an emergency assembly called by him at six o'clock in the evening, he expressed his disappointment in this generation.

Principal: "I noticed your unwillingness to defeat Ikoli, or at least, to put up a good game. I watched with disappointment how you couldn't pass the ball accurately from one end to another. And how you refused to clear the ball when it was in your end of the field, I reliably sourced information about your collective decision to abandon the games because of adequate punishment meted out to an athlete. Forgiveness is good but it doesn't take away the punishment for wrongdoing. The punishment serves as a deterrent against further commission by others. Imagine he's called back, then tomorrow it's Ephraim's turn to bully school authorities or next it's Hanatu's turn to bad-talk caféteria women. We must collectively condemn wrong and bring offenders to book regardless of friend or foe." There was grave silence. The whistling of the wind was soothing music that led to the perfect apology statement ever issued. Udoka raised his fingers up to indicate he wanted to speak, however he began to speak even before he was granted permission to speak. He spoke in a loud voice,

Udoka: "I'm sorry sir! I truly am. I'm sorry everyone. I would never have thought wrong can proceed from standing for just cause. I never knew rebellion can emanate from a desire for truth to be said. I let my temper get the best of me that unfortunate day. I can't seem to get it off my head. I don't want to be a boy that is said to have lost his placement because of bad character exhibited. I regret my actions; my mother condemned my reaction, my friends condemned my attitude. I'm so sorry, it won't happen again. To the management team, I'm deeply sorry for my actions and I wish to lead by example henceforth."

The principal as well as the school authorities and especially the National games festival department staff of the school murmured to themselves on the elevated stage they stood. They viewed his reaction as remorseful and were divided over whether or not he should be allowed to participate for qualifiers. Then shortly afterwards, the principal dismissed the assembly and warned that any body who joined in the boycotting, protesting and any kind of activity that suggests an intention to de-market the institution would mean denial of the institute's certificate. He however urged Udoka to continue to train with the team.

They all went away with mixed-feelings. The next game in hand was for the female team and adequate preparation was underway to collect all three points.

Udoka and Vera met after the assembly during a meal and they spoke at length. Vera commended Udoka for still showing support for the team even after he noticed his name was exempted from the students that made the match selection. Further inquiries were made about Tinuke. She had missed the match due to family matters she attended to. Udoka wanted to know about the success of her trip home and to personally thank her for helping him form an alliance of athletes who would keep disturbing the school management to review the ban placed on his eligibility to partake in the qualifying rounds of the games. They resolved to pay her a visit at her home if she didn't show up in camp on Sunday like she told Vera she would. This resolution became necessary as she failed to reach Vera through Mrs. Yvone as discussed.

Udoka and Vera are really getting along and there's pressure from his friends, most of whom are in their first year in the university and others running diploma programs, to ask her out on a date. He's always around and about her. They are both sixteen years old. Udoka is May born, while Vera is October born.
Vera: "Where do you see yourself in the next five years?"
Udoka: "In the next five years I'll be twenty-one years old. Wow! I don't know. I mean like I don't even know what life would be like then. You're aware trying to be rich through honest means is not really in your hands, because you cannot force anything and you are least expected to manipulate any process at any stage whatsoever. This is because you are not permitted to use force to alter natural causes. Stealing is forcefully taking anything at that very precise point when the earth hasn't rotated to arrive at that appointed and appropriated time to receive that item or items. In five years time I'll keep working hard to make this honest money for my mom and siblings so they don't feel the loss of my dad. It's not easy on them. Had and lost is worse than never had."

Vera: "I mean like, in the area of sports, the love and passion for the games; the joy of exercising daily, for love of jumpers and tracksuits all the days of your life."

Udoka: "Oh! I never really dreamed of it like that, I take the next training or match-up one at a time."

Vera: "What do you really want in life or I mean what other plans do you have assuming football doesn't work out, or God forbid you get a career threatening injury; what then?"

Udoka: "Thank you for these questions, I never thought about it this way. I always only thought about football and nothing else. I'll have to sit and think about it. Yeah! You're right, there ought to be a plan b for me. Maybe business of buying and selling; or straight up agriculture investment. I love the fields, I love grass. I think I'll think about commercial farming." he hands Vera a thumbs up and she hands him a thumbs up too and there's some human silence. The cool breeze is making the rest sounds, whistling across all corners without any holding back.

There were qualifying rounds for other sports that coming weekend. Volleyball, badminton, table-tennis and track-games with NEWLAND high school students visiting other schools and other school students visiting them in fixtures drawn up by the Lagos state ministry of sports and youth development. Vera was good at playing basketball as well as chess and she was on her way to qualifying for the National games festival in the game of chess topping the log. She's representing her school in a chess game competition. She is a great player.

At about 8:44 pm, the school's public address system was heard and names of a few students were called to receive guests at the main gate, while some others were to receive mails delivered at the school's mailbox.

Vera had three female guests accompanied by two male friends, Katab and Edidiong, rich kids who drove cars without having attained the statutory age of eighteen and without drivers licenses. The five guests were ex-students of NEWLAND high school and have gained admission to the university. They drove and parked at the parking lot by the entrance of the school. Ex-students have a leave-permit but it wasn't valid for use after six pm. Udoka, Vera and Damola, Udoka's friend in his original final year set, went to meet with the guests. They arrived at the parking lot to meet with the guest already getting along with the security men on duty. After a while the security men withdraw to their duty posts and leave the young men and women all by themselves in a quiet space.

Katab: "Anyone here wanna smoke? I got some real goodies."

"Yeah!" The lady-guests said audibly. Then he begins to prepare some smoke. In a few seconds he's done rolling a joint and he lit it up, took a couple of tokes and passed the joint to Edidiong, who also took tokes and passed to Udoka.

Udoka: "No guys! I'm good." Refusing to collect the joint which is then passed on to one of the lady guests.

Katab: "Udo why didn't you say you ain't gonna smoke when I asked, I wouldn't have rolled the whole joint in the first place."

Udoka: "What do you mean? I never replied when you asked for volunteers to smoke." Everyone chuckles.

Edidiong: "Very funny. So now you're claiming to be better than us because you don't smoke or what?"

Udoka: "I didn't say so, I'm sporting so I need my body in perfect condition. Lungs, arteries, everything needs to be in perfect condition."

Damola: "Everyone doesn't have to drink or smoke, it's not good for everyone."

Katab: "There he goes again thinking a little joint is going to hurt his game. I heard y'all lost to little Ikoli on home turf..."

Vera: "That's not why they lost."

Edidiong: "You don't know you need to get charged to play above your capacity. Don't you know herbs give nerves?"

Damola: "Not true! Certain herbs are contraband and they aren't allowed in sporting circles."

Vera: "Don't listen to them, Udoka. There's nothing to gain from smoking other than shrinking your organs."

Udoka: "Don't worry V, I know better than to start what I can't finish. Something that will consume me in the long run. Thank you Damola for looking out."

Edidiong: "Girl-boy." Referring to Udoka, "You're listening to Vera and Damola abi, cheating yourself, trying to pretend to a good boy so she can like you." he added.
Katab: "Why didn't you join the priesthood, that's where your calling is, not competitive sports." The rest burst into laughter.
Vera: "Don't listen to them." Udoka held on to his word and didn't join them in smoking. The guests chilled for a while and made their way out of the school premises. Guests can't stay in the school premises beyond ten pm. Then Vera and Udoka with Damola make their way back to the training camp.
Edidiong: "Yo! V, why are you always standing up for him?"
Vera: "He's the school captain, my captain as well."
Edidiong: "Okay! I see where we're going with this."

Sunday 12 April, 2020
12:43 pm
Mrs. Yvone called the attention of the school authorities to the accident which occurred to Tinuke and majority of the football team players sought consent from the authorities to visit her home. Misinformed, the students gathered at her house in Ikeja, singing songs and saying prayers to heal their female team captain. There they were told by Kate and Hafeez of the hospital she is in, Tagoon Hospital Ikeja. Udoka took time out and played with Salau and Hafeez for some minutes; everyone recognizes Hafeez as Tinuke's favorite sibling. Twenty-four students in total made the visit in two fourteen seater buses. They had a ten hour sick-visitation break from school. Udoka, captain of the school team, led the delegation. At the hospital entrance gate, the security men conducted thorough body temperature checks and ensured everyone wore their nose-masks appropriately. There was a mild drama when the students were accused of not keeping safe distance and that they were to break into smaller groups, which was vehemently resisted by them claiming they came as one voice and one person. Udoka, Vera, Malik and Perpetua represented the students as all of them weren't allowed into the hospital building. Tinuke was sleeping, they met with Olamilekan and Korede and sang songs of solidarity. They relayed the 'best-wishes' message from the school authorities, prayed for her quick recovery and

pledged the total support of all the athletes in the institution. Olamilekan and a tearful Korede thanked them for the love and support shown to their daughter. Olamilekan expressed regret over the game to be held in the coming weekend which Tinuke will inevitably miss. And he wished them well in their remaining qualifying activities.

Olamilekan folded a couple of one-thousand Naira bills and tried to squeeze it into Udoka's hand which he refused.

Udoka: "Sir we came empty-handed when we ought to bring fruits for her, we're unworthy to receive your support. Also I wish to personally thank you for your assistance towards recalling me to the school football team, a position I lost due to senselessness."

Olamilekan: "It's a shame we didn't meet at home, it's for the same cold soft-drinks my wife and I would have served. Please accept it, it'll gladden my heart, our hearts. I've never witnessed this large number of students visiting. It's unfortunate it's for a sad cause. But appreciate the hope that lies behind the life we all live, we hope to meet again when there's success to celebrate. May this meeting be a reminder that we owe ourselves another merrymaking hangout."

Perpetua: "When I score for the Falcons." Everyone burst into laughter, the mood was lightened. The intensity vaporized. "Amen!" They echoed.

Chapter nine.
Monday 13 April, 2020
MATHEMATICS

Emeka Umahi of Nashua memorial primary school, and five others from different primary schools made it to the final of the under-10 mathematics competition. They all qualified top of their schools under the category and were billed to compete for the top four positions who will qualify for the National games festival in under-10 mathematics challenge from Lagos state, with prize money ranging from fifty thousand - one hundred and fifty thousand Naira. The venue for the challenge is the *Ibusa* hall of the Education Resource Institute, Ikeja. The competing students were each given two invitation tickets for their parents or guardians.

It was a big day for the Umahi's as Aniete wouldn't sleep the previous night taking Emeka through several topics in his general mathematics textbook. At six o'clock in the morning, Aniete got Emeka ready and took him to the venue of the challenge where she discovered that he needed more face-masks in addition to the one wore because it was a day-long event. She returns home and prepares Ejike for them to attend the event starting at nine in the morning. Surulere to Ikeja is quite a stretch.

The venue is a large space used for receptions, meetings, seminars and public gatherings. There were six booths constructed where each contestant stood. The organizers provided writing pads and pens for solving equations. Basic mathematics questions were thrown before the contestants with all expected to solve them before choosing one in four near-possible options. A student who provides a wrong answer will have another student attempt it for bonus points. There were four girls and two boys.

9:00 am

Aniete returns with Ejike to the Education Resource Institute just in time for the challenge to begin. As they made their way into *Ibusa* hall, there was strict adherence to covid-19 regulations even though the venue didn't have many invitees.

The competition was in five stages. Two stages of forty computer base test questions in sixty minutes, two stages of five theory based questions in thirty minutes and twenty oral based questions for twenty minutes. Emeka Umahi representing Nashua memorial primary school, Surulere took off to a bright start answering the eighty computer based tests in a record seventy minutes.

At every stage-end the results would be announced and scores collated on an electronic board. The anchor of the event, Ebuka, was very friendly with the young boys and girls, cracking jokes and easing tensions.

There was a break at eleven o'clock in the morning where all the competing students as well as their guests were treated to some nice breakfast. That gave Aniete ample time to refresh Emeka and encourage him to go for the ultimate prize, the first position which he wasn't really far away from.

Emeka: "Mummy do you think I'm going to win?"

Aniete: "I don't think you're going to win, baby I believe you're going to win and make your daddy proud up there in heaven where he is."

Emeka: "I want to make my daddy proud."

Aniete: "You will, my prince. Just listen carefully to the questions before picking an answer for the oral tests. Take a look at the leaderboard, you're behind the girl from Stella high school by one point; if it stays this way, you'll qualify next to her."

Emeka: "But mummy I don't want to qualify behind her. I want to top the board."

Aniete: "Well in that case, you must ensure you don't lose any questions, and must answer theirs to gain bonus points in order to lead the pack. I trust you can do it."

Emeka: "Yes mummy, I can. Udoka didn't come?"

Aniete: "Udoka is on his way. Just concentrate. Okay!"

Emeka: "Okay mummy." Aniete's phone rings, it's vibrating. She excuses herself and takes the call.
"Hello, good morning. Yes, this is Mrs. Umahi on the phone. Oh! I'm in Ikeja at the moment. Hope there's no problem? Okay, I'm waiting for you then. Thank you too ma."
Emeka: "Mummy, who was that?"
Aniete: "Hmmm! Do you remember the police officers that came to arrest me last week?"
Emeka: "I can't forget their faces."
Aniete: "She's on her way here, she wants to discuss with me. Mr. Idris sent her to come see me."
Emeka: "All of them are on their way?"
Aniete: "No baby, she's alone."
Emeka: "I hope they don't want to trouble you today."
Aniete: "I don't know either, I hope not. I don't think so. She sounded calm, I just said I should tell you. Don't let it bother you. Okay love?" Aniete plants a kiss on Emeka's forehead.
Emeka: "Okay mummy."

The break was called off at twelve noon and the contestants mounted their booths. The competition heated up as they were entering the latter stages of the challenge. At the conclusion of the theory based questions, the leaderboard had changed significantly as three of the female competitors made the top-three while Emeka moved to fourth position. Each state of the federation will produce four candidates from the primary school division to represent the state in under-10 mathematics competition.

The female police officer attached to the Child Protection Unit of the Lagos state ministry of women affairs and infant development arrived at the Education Resource Institute and met with Aniete at the gate. Ejike was left alone in the *Ibusa* hall watching and cheering his brother on to victory.
Aniete: "Madam merely seeing your face brings bad memories to life."
"My name is Abeni." The officer replied.
Aniete: "Abeni, what brings you here?"

Abeni: "First and foremost, I want to apologize for the drama that ensued when we visited your home. In all honesty I have come to tell you that your neighbors are having a moment reporting you in our office daily. Precisely two of your elderly neighbors, I won't mention their names, but they were there that Friday we came and they were in our office this morning also."

Aniete: "My neighbors?"

Abeni: "Yes, your neighbors come to report you and your family to us, urging us to effect our constitutional mandate towards ensuring a none-fit mother isn't in-charge of children below twelve years of age. They claim you're unwell and backdate their claim to when you lost your husband. They write to us, visit frequently and I must say, they're current with the situation in your house. They know your movement, your profit and losses. You better be careful how you let people into your family affairs."

Aniete: "Hmmm! I'm speechless. I don't even know what to say. I'm afraid as well. Okay, I think I know these neighbors you're referring to. In all honesty, they were like mother and elder sister to my late husband. That flat you see is the last property my husband bought before he died. I didn't want him buying more property because I was afraid he was going to die, or perhaps leave me for another woman. It seemed at the time he was preparing to leave me, or so I felt. I believed he was gathering things to settle me with and perhaps get another woman; I feared many things. So I kept on quarreling with him over his refusal to spend more time with me. I remember warning him that all these properties he's acquiring, that I will sell them off because I wouldn't be needing them all. I told him I won't be dragging land or house with men, so I'll let them go. He would laugh and tell me how wants the best education for his sons and that was his primary reason for multiple acquisitions. He mentioned several times that Iya Jumoke and Mummy Abbey encouraged him to buy more property. These are the women I believe go to tell untrue stories about my household..."

Abeni: "Do you share your thoughts with them?"

Aniete: "Of course I do. I always tell them everything. From all the properties in Ajah and those in Enugu I sold. I take them as my husband's mother and sister. He knew them long before we met and got married. They knew his parents before they died. Who would have thought they'll go behind my back and try to take my children away from me." Aniete is freely rolling out teardrops.

Abeni: "That day, we came because your neighbors threatened our superior with a petition for failing to act on their constitutional mandate to provide and cater for infants with unstable guardians. By the way, Mr. Iliyasu has asked me to tender an unreserved apology to you for attempting to effect an arrest warrant. He returned the warrant to the magistrate and it was canceled."

Aniete: "Oh! Thank God. This is good news. So what do I do to them, I mean my neighbors?"

Abeni: "You must do nothing to them. They mustn't have a clue what I discussed with you. This is strictly confidential as it could lead to my suspension or possibly, termination of my appointment with the government; it's totally illegal to disclose a client's identity."

Aniete: "No problem Ma, you're a good woman led by good conscience, I want to assure you that no one will know about what we discussed. I'll do my best to be a good mother and friend to my children. I'll remain a helping neighbor. I won't stop doing good to others because I was treated unfairly. I'll leave it all to God."

Officer Abeni departs and Aniete returns to the hall for the rest of the competition. On entry, from the point where everyone must sanitize and wear face covering appropriately, she hears Emeka's voice from the loud speaker speaking to the people present. She begins to hasten there. She's panting. She push the giant door to the rear end of *Ibusa* hall and there he is, lights fixed on him, right there holding a microphone and a plaque having been awarded a lifetime scholarship for his strides in the area of mathematics at eight years old, and presented with a dummy cheque of one hundred and fifty thousand Naira boldly written.

"I want to thank everyone for this. My math teacher, uncle Femi, thank you. Then I want to thank my mummy in a very special way. I dedicate this award to her, and I promise her I'll make daddy proud in the National games. Love you mummy." Aniete began crying properly. Emeka and Ejike surround her and hold her tight. The other contestants came around and hit elbows with Emeka. Oluwaseyi, second position, 9 years old. Dorothy, third position, 8 years old. Mansur, fourth position, 8 years old all qualified to represent the state in the under-10 mathematics competition at the National games festival. The qualifying stages were over for all academic related activities; then the final games of the track and field events were to follow.

Chapter ten.
Wednesday 15 April, 2020
Ikeja, Lagos.
FAIRY OFF

Tinuke's injury to her collarbones neutralized her. It kept her body still and allowed her spirit freedom to roam. The mood in the house deteriorated, Hafeez is always asking to see Tinuke, which they've refused to oblige. He cries endlessly when he is refused from going to see her at the hospital, the sound draws sorrow upon their hearts.

Olamilekan and Korede drew up a visit and stay plan which involved Kate- it was Olamilekan's turn to stay up all night with Tinuke and Kate. Kate was a constant person in rendering caregiver services to Tinuke. Tinuke herself, when she wasn't asleep, she was crying.

Olamilekan sleeps either in the car or on the floor in the private-ward Tinuke is in. Kate sleeps on the floor of the ward hosting Tinuke, she was the first line of call when Tinuke needed to ease herself.

1:44 am

Olamilekan's phone vibrates in his pocket, he reaches for it and it's a bank debit alert for airtime purchase he didn't do. Upset, he leaves the room to make a call.

Olamilekan: "Babe did you buy data from my bank?"

Korede: "Yes. That's why you called?"

Olamilekan: "It's not enough to call and ask? What if it's someone else messing with my money?"

Korede: "How much did I purchase that you're breathing heavily?"

Olamilekan: "Just try and tell me before you access my account, and when I get hold of your phone, I'll delete the bank app."

Korede: "Abegi! Lemme hear word. How is my daughter?"

Olamilekan: "She's asleep."

Korede: "And Kate?"

Olamilekan: "She's fine."

Korede: "Where are you that you're quizzing me for 1k?"

Olamilekan: "I'm near the restaurant."

Korede: "I'm missing you."

Olamilekan: "Me too. Lemme go back to my duty post. Today is Wednesday. I'm not blinking an eye; lemme see if I can catch the little man they speak about." Korede laughed.

2:04 am

Olamilekan walks quietly back to Tinuke's room in the private-ward section and meets the window open. Chilly breeze finding way in. He's frightened. He's walking towards Kate, but she's fast asleep. Tinuke can't get out of her bed. Who opened the window? He thought to himself. He was perplexed, he moved over to where Tinuke lay and noticed she was smiling. He taps her legs and she doesn't respond. He pushes her legs aggressively, still she didn't even at least make any responding sign, she's smiling. At the spot he calls his wife to go and check on the boys. She rushed into their room and the window was open; this time Hafeez was smiling in his sleep.

Korede: "I tried to wake him up, but he's not responding. He's just smiling with his eyes shut."

Olamilekan: "Same here, annoyingly Kate has refused to wake up too. She's almost snoring."

Korede: "Salau wouldn't wake even if the house is on fire. I smacked him today, he was being too naughty. And I seized his PlayStation. He doesn't open his book at home again."
Olamilekan: "Let's just pray."
Korede: "Have you spoke with professor Akeredolu?"
Olamilekan: "And tell him what? Shebi you said I brought the devil to your home. I haven't called him yet, and I doubt I'm going to call him. I don't want any of your problems."
Korede: "But of all the people we spoke with over their attachment with these spirits, he's account is the only one that is close to what the boys have themselves said."
Olamilekan: "Hmmm! I didn't notice."
Korede: "I'm not joking!"
Olamilekan: "Neither am I."

There was a lot of back and forth going on between them, and while they spoke, temper brewed and tensions readily escalated. Tinuke remains on the hospital bed; bags of drip, with blood bags through needles entering and restoring her body and she's ever smiling.
Hafeez and Salau remain at home on their bed smiling. Kate is asleep. A nurse walks in to routinely check on Tinuke. She's dark-skin, wearing a face-mask revealing only rectangular eyes, a powder-blue gown resting slightly above her knee. She's carrying a tray with papers and a pen on it.
Nurse: "Hmmm! This one she's smiling, she's gisting with God o!" Olamilekan smiles as he waits by the side of the nurse. Kate is asleep.
Nurse: "We'll need more hand-gloves and more iodine. Please get more face-masks. Your daughter's guests flock in their hundreds, it's best you provide more hand sanitizer so they don't come here and infect her. Imagine if she has to combat a virus at this point in time."
Olamilekan: "God forbid. I'll buy everything. Which ones can we get immediately?"
Nurse: "None, the pharmacy hasn't opened. You'll get them later in the day. And don't open the windows to face her because she might get cold."

Olamilekan: "I didn't open the windows."
Nurse: "Hmmm! Abi it's this one here sleeping forever?"
Referring to Kate.
Olamilekan: "I don't know, I don't think so, she's been sleeping here."
Nurse: "So it's a ghost that opened it?" Olamilekan smiles and says, "Maybe!"
The nurse leaves the room after taking notes and Olamilekan continues on the phone conversation with his wife.

3:00 am
Tinuke is standing all by herself in an open area, a space wider than earth and she's hearing Hafeez' dim voice call her name repeatedly with excitement in his tone.
Tinuke: "Hafeez! Where are you? I can't see you."
Hafeez: "I'm up here. Look up Tinuke. See me here!"
Tinuke: "Where? I can't see anything." The whole area is smoky, foggy and visibility is very poor. Tinuke can hear Hafeez, but she can't see him. She's walking forward towards the sound of his voice. As his voice grew louder, she started hearing some other kids' voices, she's tensed, and she started calling Hafeez multiple times. She's walking towards the voices of what seems to be a playground for children. Then a servant appeared before her wearing a carved ivory pendant mask with no legs or hands visible; just a masked face and moving lips. She startles upon seeing him. Taken aback, she quizzes him.
Tinuke: "Who are you?"
Servant: "Chosen one, you are welcome. I'm Kadrert, servant to queen mother Idia, hostess of the assembly and I've been sent by master Hafeez to get you as we've been waiting for you. Welcome! this way please."
Tinuke: "Wait! Where is Hafeez?"
Kadrert: "He's in the presence of her majesty, the Queen mother Idia."
"Where?" Tinuke asked,
Kadrert: "Please follow me."

Kadrert, the servant, goes floating before her, leading the way. Tinuke is now in an open space, wide and far enough to be a whole state. The space was as far as her sight could travel. There are different voices, multiple

people speaking, children too. The sounds emit from underneath the fog or steam; Hafeez's voice is not hard to discern. She can't wait to see him. Kadrert: "Over there!" Hafeez screams and moves towards Tinuke, he hops on her. He has legs and arms unlike the servant Kadrert who has a carved ivory pendant mask on. Tinuke squeezes him in place of a hug; that's the physical evidence of her feeling super excited.
Hafeez: "Tinuke, everyone is waiting for you to arrive so we can go."
Tinuke: "Hold on young man, where are you hurrying to? I just arrived, will you allow me to catch my breath."
Hafeez: "Tinuke please let's go, you'll rest on the way."
Tinuke: "Let's go where?" Hafeez is pulling Tinuke towards a direction and she holds him tenaciously, not letting go of the grip.
"Queen mummy! Queen mummy!" Hafeez was screaming, excited, leading Tinuke to her.

"Welcome dear Tinuke. Your inclusion was considered undeniable as Hafeez here insists he'll enjoy the journey alongside you; we agree with him." Tinuke heard from the bottom of the floor-less under where mist is rising. Everyone is floating, the area is vaporized.
Tinuke: "What are we looking like? and what feeling is this? Having legs we can't walk with as I see no floor, having hands that can't handle anything else but Hafeez. Where is this place? Who are you?"
"I'm Queen Idia, mother of Esigie, Oba of Benin. We are in a ciborium, a keep for free people; your astroperson is present here with us. Young people are free by their minds being void of adulteration. Young persons are tools for truth, sandals for moral matching. All minds have assembly points, it's called consciousness. Young minds meet here. We are higher spirits who exist in a realm within realms where we wait for the end of all time. We're in a space where we look forward to the future and take steps to correct or amplify yesterday for the greater good of tomorrow. A final time is set by the Father of spirits for all of mankind to cease; we're spirits made out of human creativity and experience. That time for man's ending is known to Him alone. We however are in the waiting-world where we exist in non-human form but have and hold our human physique, identities and statuses because we haven't been completely dislodged from our bodily forms. We retain the age, looks and stature of our death, unperturbed by human limitations. Mankind hasn't stopped existing; so until the end of time, we wait."

Tinuke: "What is this mission?"

Queen Idia: "It's a warning mission. It's a journey back in time to correct the problem that led to the greatest heist in man's history. The scramble and partition of Africa. You see, hundreds of years ago, a certain King and ruler of a tremendously great and wealthy empire sought to go on pilgrimage to the holy city. This great King, Mansa Musa along with thousands of his servants announced Africa as they traveled from Mali through Egypt to the holy city. His entourage consisted of hundreds of private musicians, thousands of male and female servants who carried thousands of pounds gold bars and other equipment, camels carrying pounds of gold-dust that the price of gold crashed in the world market of old, this action of he's and his people beamed light on the black race and created interest from outsiders. That voyage clad in gold made it to the Catalan Atlas decades after his trip. The resulting effect from that trip is Europeans who at that time were facing population decline, unrest, famine, the Black Plague and series of uncertainties started grouping and showing up in Africa in search of gold and precious metals. Years after, to the present day, these precious metals have become a curse to us Africans. Criminal European monarchs illegally mined and impoverished Africa, looting and stealing her mineral resources. Exchanging precious metals for ammunition, while installing envy and hatred amongst the victims. Had Musa not announced African wealth, the poor and starving Europe wouldn't have invaded Africa. At least not in a time where African military might have not become sophisticated. The British military with support from the British crown destroyed the Benin kingdom, my kingdom, and carted away our physical artifacts with spiritual linkages. Same was done to several other empires and kingdoms. Africa is doomed because of Europe. This mission seeks to restore an awareness culture amongst young blacks to realize the strength that lies beneath their dark skins."

Tinuke: "Wow! I never thought of it this long. How come they don't teach African history in-depth in classes?"

Queen Idia: "Because they simply don't want you to have a yesterday older than the one they created for you to know and believe. They chose the slavery era to start African history to wipe out their atrocities committed against vulnerable black people. Also to perfect the narrative that blacks are inferior."

Tinuke: "Why are the sophisticated blacks of the west not a part of these movements alongside us?"

Queen Idia: "Simply said, the black-race in the west is a lost cause. A closed door. They consider themselves white, not being blacks at all. Always trying to force themselves to be where the original inhabitants don't want them to be. Always wishing equality with a host that clearly doesn't want them around. The Jews in the west built the territory of Israel. Yet the blacks in the west have deserted Africa. Claiming they don't belong here when we can see from the color of their flesh that they don't belong there. Hence, the spirits of great African ancestors have begun recruiting blacks resident in Africa to restore Africa to where she belongs as the home of civilization."

Tinuke: "Ookay! So does Hafeez know exactly what to do or say when he goes before the Mansa?"

Queen Idia: "The spirits of his ancestors who need no more of the suffering and misery of African children will be with him and speak for him. They will lead you both and have you both return safely."

Tinuke: "What's time travel like?"

Queen Idia: "Time travel is the conveyance of persons or objects or other core components of earth from one era to another. It is a mode of transportation where the body isn't needed in the case of persons traveling; unless the traveler has need for human body when he arrives at his destination then his body will fall into particles of sand, tinier than dust, rise up to the sky spinning around very fast with the speed of sound or even faster. In other words my dear, and so I do not confuse you, your astroperson, that is your spirit woman is sufficient for any trip in between time, but if you need to do physical work at your destination, then your physical person will join buy reducing into fine particles of dust and through high winds similar to mini-tornadoes, your body's fast spinning particles will go up and suspend in the skies; then at the point of you're arrival- your destination, fine particles of sand smaller or tinier than dust will piece together and form the body where your astroperson will dwell for the period of your stay. In your case my dear, we had to present you with a fall and a temporal injury to neutralize your body in order to perform this task without blemish as both your spirit and body are required; and where else is fitting for your rest than in the hive of family. That's why your accident happened indoors." Tinuke is quiet, pondering all by herself.

"Speak my dear, what is this doubt within you?" Queen mother Idia said, "What about my parents? My mom; will she be alright? My dad too. And when will my fractured bones heal? I heard you say my accident was premeditated, what happens to my dream of playing professional football?" Tinuke asked,

Queen Idia: "You worry about your body, you forget it was assigned to your soul for carrying out human activities. Identify the activities and tasks of your soul and ensure your body carries them out while you still possess a body. Be informed that there are some greater activities of the soul the body isn't aware of. Also there are some activities of the body the soul is dearly interested in. Either way, there is an action required by either body or soul, or by both. In this instance, your spirit and body are needed for this task, which is to accompany a faithful servant to and from the past. For the record, note that your body can't stay for eternity based on the material used for making it. It is therefore pertinent to achieve all the tasks, activities, roles, assignments requested from your body before your soul departs from it. You'll be dead much longer, your body will lie in the darkness of a grave and your soul will exist in torment if you fail to carry out the things you have been assigned in this lifetime; there are things your soul will love to achieve now that it has a body. Do those things now. The wise don't need passages, a word is sufficient."

Tinuke: "When do we depart?"

Queen Idia: "Patience my dear, you must be prepared for this. The mastery of the rotation and revolution of earth is key to time-travel; astrodynamics also. Earth isn't static, so as it revolves and rotates, the pupil of time-travel must be vigilant as a slight error may have you end up in an undeserved time and an untamed place. Dearest, all energy emanate from the sun and the moon. Also, you must understand that earth's magnetic field along with tidal forces of the moon and sun, the solar flares can disrupt time-travel. These forces cannot be denied as they form a monumental part of existence. Over here, milliseconds or error or miscalculation can transfer a traveler years away from his original intended destination."

Tinuke: "What's earth's magnetic field?"

Queen Idia: "They are magnetic fields that flow from the earth's interior out into space where it meets and interacts with the solar winds; these are a stream of charged particles emanating from the sun; like I mentioned, all energy comes from the moon and the sun. You need to read up on all these things on the internet."

Tinuke: "Okay! When do we get back, I mean at what time would we return home?"

Queen Idia: "My dear, the Father of spirits created time, He exists not by it. Accountability began when time started. Who is the Father of spirits accountable to? Certainly none as none is greater or equal to Him. All spirits, greater or lower work and live within time; however for higher dimension spirits, time is simply a flat board, a slate. Just continually storing and recording itself; saving all activities and naming the different storage folders. Time is rolling like a camera hung up on a wall at a speed of twenty-four hours a day. The Father of spirits alone knows what time, we can only infer without full proof of what will be based on the seasons. For the period you will have in the past, you shall know red or orange skies. And after your mission is accomplished, the skies shall turn brown; then the gatekeeper is ready to open the gates between times and let you out of that era and back to your present day. The time to return is when you have convinced the Mansa that he ought not to announce unready Africa, because all what Africa possesses she is unable to protect them for herself. These looters, the European armies are better equipped and their monarchs are soulless supporting crooks who approved deceits, looting, maiming, and criminality in their attitude of conquests."

Tinuke: "Wow o'wow!"

Queen Idia: "Repeat after me-
        In turns in turns we go
        In turns in turns we go
        Return shall be, then condescension shall cease
        Good fortune it is for them who proclaim to see
        Noble is the heart of the servants, success is their will

Tinuke: In turns in turns we go
        In turns in turns we go
        Return shall be, then condescension shall cease
        Good fortune it is for them who proclaim to see
        Noble is the heart of the servants, success is their will

Queen Idia: "Recite these words continually without end holding each other and the process of **Mpkosa** will be initiated. You must be together

74

at all times so the magical powers will cover you both and deliver you where you collectively choose."

Queen mother Idia takes Tinuke on a tour of the ciborium and she experiences the rest of the recruits for the different journeys to the past. There Tinuke is introduced to Queen Amina, Queen Moremi and a host of greatly revered queens and kings of black descent who lived lives worthy of emulation. A date was set for the commencement of the trip back in time. Hafeez as well as other young boys and girls have been recruited to go back in time for different reasons to meet and convince different people to do or omit to do certain acts for the greater good of the black race.

5:30 am

The nurse returns to Tinuke's room for a routine check. Kate is awake and Olamilekan is too. She insists on the hand-gloves and face-masks which Olamilekan personally instructs her to write a list of all the items that will be needed for better care of his daughter. At seven o'clock in the morning, Korede came to replace Kate and Olamilekan. She brought food and drinks for the nurses and security men on duty. Olamilekan and Kate returned home to Salau and Hafeez who are in safe hands of Usman.

As soon as Olamilekan enters his house he goes into his sons and sees if the window is open. And it was wide open so he called Hafeez to himself and talked with him.

Olamilekan: "My boy, come over here. How come I noticed you don't join Salau to play games."

Hafeez: "Daddy Salau is always cheating me. When it's my turn to score him, he'll pause the game and play it again, then I'll play the ball wide. Even when we're racing, he'll pause the game when I'm in a bend, when I'm about to turn my motorbike on a corner, that's how the rider will fall off his motorbike."

Olamilekan: "Salau, that's unfair cheating on your brother like that." Salau chuckles.

Salau: "I'll win him even if I don't do that. And daddy it's because he can't play that's why he's saying all those things. Okay daddy come let's play."

Olamilekan: "Ah! I don't know how to play o! Leave me out of this, I'll watch you guys." Hafeez is interested in watching his father play against Salau. He'll support anyone who defeats Salau, his tormentor.

Hafeez: "Daddy play, daddy play with him and win him for me. I'll support you all the way." he's excited, he's running all over the place. Salau hands a controller to Olamilekan and they begin to race. Hafeez is super thrilled. He's up and down the couch.

After three races, Salau wins all which make him jubilant. He's boasting. After the dust settled, Olamilekan offered to take the boys out to lunch. Kate is instructed to get ready as they'll return to the hospital later to relieve Korede from her duty post.

Olamilekan and his sons drive to a fast-food outlet and choose to eat-in.

Olamilekan: "Hi, please I want Jollof rice and fried-rice, make it two portions and coleslaw. I'd like some drum-sticks too; bottle water will do. Guys, what do you want to have?"

Salau: "I want Jollof rice and moi-moi and turkey and ice-cream and cola drink."

Olamilekan: "Hafeez, what do you want to eat?"

Hafeez: "I want only ice-cream." they, all three males ferry their trays to a corner Hafeez chose and began merrymaking.

3:55 pm

Olamilekan: "Hafeez, were you with your friends today? I noticed your window was open when I walked in this morning." Hafeez smiled and didn't respond.

Salau: "Daddy, they told him not to tell anyone anything. Especially you and mummy."

Hafeez: "It's a lie, Salau you can lie o!"

Salau: "I'm not lying. I heard them tell him."

Olamilekan: "Hafeez are you lying to your daddy?"

Hafeez: "No! Kadrert said no one needs to know when we're leaving for the Mali empire." Surprised, Olamilekan said, "Going to where? Mali? For what? With whom? Who are we?"

Salau: "Him and Tinuke."

Olamilekan: "How is that even possible? Tinuke is bedridden, she can't even play football for maybe three to four months..."

Hafeez: "She doesn't need her body to go to Mali. Her willing soul is sufficient to go and return before you even know it."
Olamilekan: "Have you told your mother?"
Hafeez: "No dad. She'll say no. Kadrert mentioned to her precisely that she'll panic and vehemently oppose it."
They ate in Western Fried Chicken, a top spot in Ikeja and had drinks too. Olamilekan bought takeaway meals for Kate, Usman and his wife. On their way to the parking lot Hafeez cried out, "Daddy carry me!"
Olamilekan: "No, I'm not carrying you. When I'm asking you questions you're not answering me; walk!"
Hafeez: "Daddy carry me please. My shoes are hurting my legs."
Olamilekan: "Tell the Queen to carry you."
Hafeez: "Daddy it's for your own good I'm not telling you everything."
Salau: "Oops, he just spilled it out!"
Olamilekan: "What did you just say? That's its for my own good?" Hafeez is quiet and he walks on by himself to the back seat of the car.
"Did he just say for my own good?" Olamilekan whispered. With Salau in the passenger seat, Olamilekan humbly drove back home.

Olamilekan and Kate prepare and depart for the hospital. They arrived after mild traffic especially on Ajao road and met Korede at the reception.
Olamilekan: "Babe do you know the latest? I am afraid of Hafeez. That's not a boy anymore o. Imagine a small-rat said he's not telling me anything about the mystery persons for my own good."
Korede: "No, he did not."
Olamilekan: "My dear he did, twice. Without remorse. As in, the little man didn't pity me that I'm his father. I wanted to squeeze him; as in slap his mouth. But I still just cool down before those queen guys target me. I didn't utter a word."
Korede: "I'm going to smack him, it's getting out of hand."
Olamilekan: "No, smack Salau. Salau said 'oops', as in, after Hafeez said it was for my own good he's keeping stuff away from me, Salau said something something spilled it out, as in, that

Hafeez has told me it's for my own good. I mean like it's supposed to be a secret."

Korede: "In that case, I'll change the package for them, I'll tie my face for them."

Olamilekan: "Just smack them, two of them know things. That will do the trick. As in, use force so they can tell us all that is going on. Severely I've thought about Tinuke's injury being a making of these evil people the boys are speaking about. I mean how can someone just fall down and break their neck. Where does that happen? Imagine we're referring to a goalkeeper. A team captain. I'm slowly losing my mind. Babe smack these boys once and for all."

Korede: "Relax my love, calm down. It's not every time you smack a child, you have to let that child know there are other forms of deprivations for disobeying orders. Restrict them access to things and places strictly for a stretch of time. In fact smacking a child is wrong, it hardens the child. Children only need communication. Just leave them to me."

Olamilekan: "Yes na, that's for godly children, normal children. We're dealing with children that are possessed. Children that dine with the devil..."

Korede: "Watch your mouth and what you say about your own children."

"Baby you're slimming down. See your neck is showing. I wish I can take all the pressure away from you. My chubby bunny is losing weight. I guess you don't have an appetite." Olamilekan said, holding his wife in his arms.

"I do, but most times when I look at my children my tongue gets bitter and I don't want to eat anymore." Korede replied.

"I'll get a food supplement for you. I'll ask Ovie the one you should take; that would force you to eat. Don't worry, they'll be okay. So far there haven't been any threats to life. Just a mystery journey they all claim is for the betterment of Africa. I know my children, as adults we will be proud to be the ones saddled with the task of black mental liberation."

Korede: "I'll be glad to being their mother. Wait! When did Doctor say her next surgery is?"

Olamilekan: "I think he said tomorrow, I'll ask him again. Nurse said we'll need to buy plenty more things o. She was just mentioning many things. I gave her the go-ahead to purchase everything."

Chapter eleven.
Saturday 18 April, 2020
MORE GAME TIME

The first of three qualifying matches for the female football category was underway with NEWLAND high queens, Agege hosting the defending champions of the category, St. Bridget's girls secondary school, Victoria Island. The game was tense from the moment the groups were formed. Group D, touted as the group of death, have Pace College, NEWLAND high queens, St. Bridget's and Fountain Ladies football club. The team lineup didn't have their captain, Tinuke, which was considered a bad omen. Esther Rilwan was added in place of Tinuke Ajose.

3:00 pm
The match got off to a bright start with the home team passing the ball around and holding on to possession. The principal of NEWLAND high was really impressed with the movement of the ball by his female football team. The players on the pitch as

well as the coaches were in high spirits. The few students and die-hard football officials allowed into the mini-stadium were all wearing face-masks and there were hand washing machines and sanitizer at close points in the premises; there were nose-masks but they were for sale.

The first second-look incident in the match occurred in the ninth minute, when Oluwatosin Sadiq of the visitor's team fired a long range shot which ricocheted off the crossbar; the second-choice goalie wasn't anywhere close to the ball. The resultant goal-kick brought about good footballing from the home-side and they looked more confident passing the ball around and holding on to it longer as well as going forward.

The heat of the sun was causing dehydration which forced the center-referee to call for a five minutes rehydration break at thirty-minutes into the game; water was taken by some of the girls and the match officials.

The five minutes rehydration break seemed to remove the flow of the game from the home-side as the visitors took control of the game for the rest of the first half. On the stroke of halftime, Kemi Wellinton of St. Bridget struck the ball hard with her right foot which deflected off the side of a NEWLAND high queen's player and into the back of the net, sending the goalkeeper the wrong way for the first goal of the match. Breaths ceased. Then there was loud screaming of 'goal' from the visiting team's less than fifteen supporters. The few of them scattered around with nose-masks jubilated aggressively and some of the students on the substitute bench ran onto the field of play in celebration of the goal scored. The referee blew the whistle for halftime after three minutes of added time.

During the halftime break, Udoka and the team management sought to restore confidence in the players. Udoka reminded them that a teammate was injured and that a good result against St. Bridget would aid her recovery. They talked to the girls on confidence and passing the ball short, to the nearest woman. Then came the principal. He stood with them in the dressing room but didn't utter a word, he was gazing at the school's crest engraved on the floor, in marble, in the middle of the dressing room. There were several formation changes as they reverted to 4-3-3 formation and two substitutions were made.

The second half of the game started with the visitors on the driving seat. They came out blazing from both flanks consolidating on their 4-5-1 formation. Their pace and accurate passes helped them break the host defense multiple times until a free-kick was awarded to the host team against the run of play, for a rough tackle from a visiting midfielder on Abimbola Rauf. The resultant free-kick was the ball in the back of the net from a few yards out which leveled the scores at one goal each. The visitor's goalkeeper was a spectator, as she stood and watched the perfectly taken free-kick curl and drop in the back of the net. As expected, there was wild jubilation from the home supporters, the girls ran wild in joyful celebration. Yes they'd scored the defending champions and were even more confident going forward. It was soothing. As the second half progressed, they witnessed more aggressiveness and tougher handling of each other. However, both teams became stronger and played better football. Then came a second goal for the visitors when the ball was moved from the left flank and the combination of Yewande and Jolie put pressure on the host's right-back, Teni Ajumoh. There was constant flow of the ball on that left flank through perfect passes and it eventually paid off when the visitors squared a good cross from the left and an erroneous collision of heads of two NEWLAND high queen's central defenders laid the ball at the foot of Kemi Wellinton, who make no mistake in placing the ball in the back of the net. This was embarrassing for the defenders, especially the clash of heads. There was another wild jubilation by the visitors. Their hard work paid off. The second goal was surely demoralizing for the hosts.

In the eighth minute, the host team got a free-kick right in front of the visitors six-yard box and a second yellow card for the visitor's captain, Jewel Isong; the card reduced the visitors to ten ladies against eleven. The host anticipated a goal from the free-kick to at least even the scores. The free-kick was poorly taken and the ball didn't go past the visitor's wall of players, much to the disappointment of the host's coaching team.

"What a waste." They muttered.

At five minutes to the final whistle, the home team pushed for a goal that could force a point out of the match. They attacked the visitors from all angles, playing long-balls into the penalty area but yielding no results.

The one-man advantage didn't count for something as the visitors added a third goal to seal the victory and take all three points. The defeat was hard to take; two NEWLAND high queens were spotted crying after the game. The injury to their captain capped the misery as some of the players from St. Bridget were making provocative remarks while celebrating their victory.

This defeat was the second the school had experienced in the last one week of qualifiers. Later that day, and as it was custom, the principal called an assembly to discuss the game played and the rest of the qualification matches ahead.

A few hours later, all the student-athletes were gathered together when the principal, in company with the school's guardian and counsellor arrived at the assembly ground. They wore their face-masks as they greeted the students.

Principal: "You, at the back, yes you! Put your face-mask properly. Ladies and gentlemen, Kings and Queens, I wish to express my dissatisfaction with the games our prestigious school athletes have played. Today's game is nothing short of abysmal. Kings and Queens do better; they push themselves extra for the sake of the crown. I must state that we understand the loss of key players and that the match was against a really good side, but failing to score in a home game hits differently. I want to plead that we take the remaining qualifying matches seriously so as to get a spot at the festival..."

Students: "We want Udoka! We want Udoka! We want Udoka!" The over one hundred student-athletes were screaming at the top of their voices, holding their fists to the sky.

Principal: "I thought I mentioned he's matter is under review and we'll communicate with him and his family shortly." But the students screamed even more.

Principal: "May I remind you of the riot act I read out to you a week ago." Unperturbed, they screamed louder and the guardian and counsellor pulled the principal by his jacket slightly and whispered to him. This move caused the students to raise their voices and their fists higher.

Mrs Igbokwe: "Dear students I want you to sing a song with me, and she started singing 'Solidarity forever, solidarity forever!'" they sang and sang along.

Mrs Igbokwe: "After careful review of the circumstances that led to the just and appropriate punishment meted out to Udoka Umahi and the days that followed, taking into consideration his level of remorse; I wish to, on behalf of the school management and the entire staff of NEWLAND high welcome back Udoka Umahi to the school athletics team and remind him of the role of captain he's holding, his need to lead by example and finally charge him to take the male and female teams to the National games in Edo state and bring back all the medals."

The school's assembly ground shook. The students ran amuck. Udoka who stood at the rear started crying, Vera shed tears too. There was louder screaming. Udoka has been recalled to the team. The celebration seemed like they won the gold medal already.

Principal: "Quiet! Ladies and gentlemen, let me use this rare moment to express how I feel about this school; this ideology called NEWLAND high school. In 2002 I applied for consent to establish this place to serve as an optimum academic resource center, but the state government refused my request for several reasons. Well, one of the unwritten reasons is that politicians in the ministry of education were not very comfortable with an individual owning an institution of learning; me precisely. They reasoned that my ideals of life, if impacted on students, would lead them to communist state of reason. Communism is in itself not a bad system of affair, the only thing is that it isn't practicable in a multi ethnic state like ours. However in our own case we're practicing democracy which isn't properly crafted; don't forget democracy is majority, not logic or reasonable; just numbers. Communism is togetherness, it's for and about one people. What you exhibited a few minutes ago is togetherness, oneness. A community of students stood up for one of yours. I am hopeful that the years ahead will bring us good tidings. Lastly, I wish to inform all of us that I will be proceeding to retirement in the coming days. I'll be seventy years old in the coming weeks and I believe I am unfit to lead a bunch of teeming youths. We're concluding plans to name a replacement before the beginning of the games festival. I urge all of you to take your academic work seriously as you are doing with your athletic works. Udoka, wear your masks properly, will you? As you have witnessed, the students and staff place our faith in your abilities. Make us proud. Thank you all so much and have a restful weekend."

The celebration for Udoka's recall continued, it seemed to diminish the effects of the defeats suffered. They returned to the training camp and started more intense preparations for the next games in the football category as well as the basketball category. Udoka, Jasper, Vera and Perpetua gathered together for a brief meeting where they finalized the players to be fielded for the last two games for both male and female category. At the end of the compilation, names were forwarded to the team management for final verification and approval.

Through Mrs. Yvone, the students reached out to Mr. And Mrs. Ajose, inquiring about Tinuke and her level of recovery. The students also told the Ajoses' that Udoka has been recalled and would participate in the rest of the games. The Ajoses' we're glad that Tinuke's friends were still keeping in touch with her despite being absent from school.

Chapter twelve.
Sunday 19 April, 2020
Waiting-World

The ceremony to inaugurate the committee to voyage back in time on a mission to correct the past in order to better advance the present day began with nomination of persons and designation of roles. This exercise was largely fruitful. The star point of the event was the moment to choose the messenger to visit the Shonghai empire and prepare their army for sophisticated wars in the desert.
The messenger for the voyage to Mansa Musa of Mali is Hafeez Ajose and his guardian-at-voyage is Tinuke Ajose. The messengers for the kingdoms of Ife, Nri; the Ghana, Benin, Mali, Oyo, Jolof, Wolof, and

Bornu empires of Western Africa were already agreed upon and were about to be commissioned.

Drums are beating, trumpets blasting, divine hymns are being sung. A procession of millions of ancestors march on and lead a league of messengers and guardians-at-voyage to the place of departure, a point where they travel to separate destinations chosen for them. Floating on misty substance and singing hymns to the Father of spirits, they marched on to realize and experience a time of long awaiting. A time of genuine and total emancipation from mental slavery, as none but ourselves can free our minds.

Queen Idia: "We're about to witness a historic moment where our history is rewritten. A time where we fight from yesterday having had exclusively the privilege of witnessing today for an awesome tomorrow and beyond. The Benin kingdom is proud to initiate this process of revisiting and rewriting time-past. This task is enormous, this task is possible, doable too. Heroes of this race, fighters of this kind; the black kind, I speak to you and your further-selves, do you always and be you always!

With the powers vested on me by the General-assembly of ancestors of our kind, I hereby declare this mission of redemption open and I charge all messengers and guardians to achieve the targets set out in the communique issued at the close of that assembly. May the just will of the Father of spirits and the spirits of our ancestors be with your spirits and guide you and your guardians.

But first, we must test the will of the guardians of the messengers. We must be fully convinced that you guardians are the best for the supporting roles assigned to you and that you all are ready in truth for the success of the mission. Hence, there shall be a test, after which, if convinced, you shall be duly certified."

At once, there were fairy instances where the messengers and their guardian-at-voyage were placed before different life circumstances and are left to make decisions choosing from options available to them from occurrences playing out.

It happened that Tinuke had a dream where she witnessed her brother Hafeez been sent on an errand to deliver a parcel to Ibadan, and it happened that Salau was sent with him. She was disturbed by the task delegated for a baby and Salau, equally an infant and then she protested. The sender insisted that Hafeez in company with Salau begin delivery of the parcel at once. Without an option and without her mobile phone to reach her parents, she forced Salau home and she quickly joined Hafeez in a bus to Ibadan, the Oyo state capital. At a stop before cocoa house, there were men clad in military uniforms seemingly on a stop-and-search mission. Tinuke grabbed hold of the parcel Hafeez was carrying and hid it between her body and the side of the bus; she covered it further with her scarf. The military men stood at a distance and called out Hafeez three times. Tinuke and Hafeez were terrified, they were visibly shaken. Then they called out Hafeez another set of three times, and threatened to shot at everyone in the bus if Hafeez doesn't show up. The rest passengers in the bus muttered, they warned that they'll expose them both instead of to lose everyone- that it is better for one to die, than for all to be lost. At this moment, Tinuke said in a loud voice, "I'm Hafeez." Then she was lifted and taken to the door of the bus by hands which appeared from under the bus seats. There, a faceless male figure adorned with gold and silver ranks in military vest appeared before her, then smells her body and declares, "This is not the boy!" rejected, then she was lifted up and taken back to her seat where she was with Hafeez. What seemed to be light as bright as the sun divided into two and became two bright lights and rested on the face of the male figure in military vest and shone on the passengers with fury, then the rest of the passengers begin booing and clapping at them aggressively, they then attempt to snatch Hafeez, but Tinuke threw the parcel at them, withdrew Hafeez who was crying and distracted them and then she woke up.

11:33 am
Tagoon hospital, Ikeja.

Tinuke's eyes opened freely for the first time since her fall, to the surprise of everyone in the room. She called Hafeez severally with the little energy reserved in her. Korede rushed to her bed side and comforted her saying, "He's fine. He's at home." "Where's Salau?" She inquired, "He's fine, he's with Kate and Usman. They are all fine."
Tinuke: "Mummy what happened?"

Korede: "My love, you and your brother were playing when you slipped and fell, you hurt your body severely and shifted your collarbone. You've undergone two successful surgeries, the second which was completed eleven hours ago. So I'm supposed to be surprised you are awake. But because I've not encountered stranger moments in my life, I'm only thankful to God and I'll not question anything anymore." Tinuke smile.

"Hello baby, she has woken up, matter of fact she's talking with me. That's what I'm telling her she just had a surgery. Okay I'm waiting. No I haven't, you tell him. Love you." Korede spoke with her husband on the phone.

Tinuke: "Where's daddy?"

Korede: "He's close by. He went to buy some antibiotics for quick healing of the surgery cuts."

Tinuke: "Mummy I had a dream, Hafeez was there too when..."

Korede: "Baby you need to rest, we can talk about your dream later. You underwent a surgery that lasted three hours. You really need to rest."

Tinuke: "Mummy I've been resting my body is aching."

Korede: "I claim your healing, you are healed and restored in Jesus name." Tinuke smiles and responds, "Amen."

Tinuke: "Have we played St. Bridget?"

Korede: "Yes baby, you guys did exceptionally well; everyone was proud of your teammates. You will surely defeat Pace college, by four goals or more. I can assure you. Just relax my love, everything is fine." Holding her arm tight and rubbing her hair. Sobbing.

Tinuke: "Who's in goal for us?"

Korede: "Hmmm! Baby, this other girl was in goal for you; what's her name? And she did a lot of saves on behalf of the team, that's why you girls will defeat Pace college in your next match. Baby I want to inform you that all your friends have been checking on you and can't wait for you to heal and get back to the squad."

Tinuke: "They are?"

Korede: "Yes love, they wouldn't miss any second to say hi and wish you well." Tinuke is smiling and she falls asleep. Korede would not leave her side, she's mostly hiding the fact that she's crying from her daughter.

87

Chapter thirteen
Wednesday 22 April, 2020
NEWLAND high school, Agege, Lagos
I LIKE VERA

Udoka: "Dave, abeg gimme leg make I follow momci reason for Aunty Yvone side. We tok nine o'clock in the morning."
David: "From there I go come back hostel o! No be say, yu go say make I escort yu go girl's hostel."
Udoka: "Cool down! Once we tok wit momci, we don fall back. E no good make only one pesin make waka."
David: "I don tell you."
Udoka: "Dave my man, cool down. Las las na to say hi to Vera. Nothing much."
David: "I don tell you, from Aunty Yvone side I de return hostel."
"But guy, you sabi say I like am." Udoka said, as he and his friend David Ohama, a badminton player, and also a fellow returnee from the previous school-academic set take a walk to a school staff premises.
"All man sabi say you like am. Yu don virtually tell everybody say yu like am. But yu don tell her say yu like her? No!" David replied, fixing his du-rag under the head-warmer he's wearing.
Udoka: "Guy, take it easy, I'm only sixteen, you don't expect me to be all swift and stuff overnight. I don't yet have all the necessary skills to pull off a first successful job just yet. I mean you don't expect me to be a pro in a minute. Breathe guy, breathe."
David: "Imagine, everyone knows you like her because you told them, but you haven't told the girl herself. She doesn't even know you like her."
Udoka: "Bro, slow-down, she doesn't have to know I like her for me to go on and like her. As in? Am I missing something? Me and my likeness again? I like her, final. I don't need her permission, or anyone else's consent to like her. I like Vera."
David: "So you came back because of Vera?"

Udoka: "I don't know. I don't just want those little boys talking to her; so I'm telling everyone to run along; or at least while I'm here every little Hommie steer clear."

They arrived at Aunty Yvone's and Udoka got on her phone to talk with his mother. He takes a walk a few meters away from a staff-block with Aunty Yvone's phone.

Udoka: "Mummy how are you?"

Aniete: "I'm glad my lovely son. My heart is pleased. Your brother made us proud, he won himself a spot at the National games for junior mathematics category. Baby they gave us fifty thousand Naira for preparation. He's name, your brother's name is in the newspapers. The world has seen my son's name on the national dailies. I am happy, I feel fulfilled."

Udoka: "Hello, mummy, I can't hear you."

Aniete: "My baby I can hear you, loud and clear."

Udoka: "Mom, what did you say? Network is poor over here."

Aniete: "Never mind! When is your next game coming up?"

Udoka: "This Saturday and upper Saturday."

Aniete: "Hope you're preparing adequately and hope you're staying out of trouble?"

Udoka: "Yes mom."

Aniete: "What's wrong? Are you alright? Why are you sounding down? Is there something bothering you?"

Udoka: "No mom, I'm fine. Just that; can I tell you something?" he's still walking away, needing exclusive privacy.

Aniete: "Of course, my husband, speak to me, I'm all ears."

Udoka: "Okay, mom there's this girl l like and."

Aniete: "And what?"

Udoka: "I don't know, I like her."

Aniete: "Okay darling, what's her name?"

Udoka: "Vera."

Aniete: "Beautiful name. So, have you told Vera you like her, and what did she say?"

Udoka: "Okay I was about to, but. But do I really have to tell her, I mean, she sees how I'm all over her and how I always check on her, and..."

Aniete: "So Vera is all you do in school training camp?"

Udoka: "No mom, of course not. It's just that I like her, that's all. No big deal about it."
Aniete: "You will have to tell her how you feel, so you will know how she feels about you."
Udoka: "Okay mom, but before I forget; you know my friend Tinuke? Yes mom, the one I told you had an accident at home. So we went to pay her a visit. School gave us ten hours and two buses. So a few of us went and her father gave us money. We refused, but he insisted and when we tendered the money in school, the admin officer, Aunty Fidelia said we should keep it. I asked the house on what method to use to share it amongst ourselves and they all elected that I kept all the money. Twenty thousand Naira. Honestly mummy he tried. He really did well. The money is in my locker. Okay mom, I'll be careful.
Exactly, just go there and appreciate him, use the opportunity to visit her. Tell her we wish her well. I know, I think she should have either gone for her second operation or she'd have had it. I'll send the address to you; go now, please. Love you mom. I will, I promise. Yes mom."
Udoka burst into laughter and hung up the call. He's walking back to the staff-block and waiting for David.

Tagoon hospital
Ikeja, Lagos

3:22 pm
Dr. Ovie: "You mean you went to FGC Asaba? Then I must have missed you by a second. I graduated from FGC Asaba as the overall worst student. Everybody's score, every performance was better than mine. I was known in all the secondary schools in the area I ended up studying for failing every test, every everything. I repeated SS3 two times."
Aniete: "Oh my gosh! And he's so serious saying it." Laughing uncontrollably,
Dr. Ovie: "No need lying about it, I'm a surgeon today. It's good for people to know they are entitled to give themselves second chances at whatever they want to have or be."

Aniete: "Third chances, maybe. I'm just happy the way you admitted doing poorly in school. I did averagely. In class I sat in the middle, not in front or at the rear. I was an average student." Olamilekan joins them in front of the room, watching Tinuke through a glass window.
Olamilekan: "I'm sorry for taking longer, more papers to sign, ultimately I used the restroom."
Aniete: "That's okay!"
Dr. Ovie: "Hope you washed that your hand properly?" They laugh out loud.
Olamilekan: "Yu de mad."
Aniete: "Once again, thank you for everything, especially the money my son got from your generosity. We're grateful. And may God heal your child, as a mother I can imagine what you're going through firsthand."
Olamilekan: "He didn't have to tell you or anyone else. It was an honor and privilege to welcome them. I saw young people with strength and desire to improve their bodies, I envied them. At their age, I was best connected with vices. I had to appreciate them. Imagine, they came to lift a compatriot from the sickbed to join them in the battlefield. I almost shed a tear."
Aniete: "She'll be fine."
Olamilekan: "I have no doubt in my mind. She will be strong again. She opens her eyes now, there's movement of her neck. All thanks to God. Credit to this friend of mine and Doctor of the year, Ovie my guy." Ovie chuckles.
Aniete: "My regards to your wife, I'll be on my way now."
Olamilekan: "She'll hear. Hopefully, we'll meet on the last qualifying match day. Udoka invited me."
Aniete: "I'll look forward to that day. Have a great day."
Dr. Ovie: "Bye!"
Olamilekan: "Bye!"

Aniete Umahi departs from the hospital. Olamilekan is expecting Korede to relieve him and sleepover with Tinuke.
Dr. Ovie: "Guy, wassup?"
Olamilekan: "I de, wetin de?"
Dr. Ovie: "I need Prof. details."

Olamilekan: "Which Prof.?"

Dr. Ovie: "Prof. Akeredolu."

Olamilekan: "Based on what? Guy wetin de sup?"

Dr. Ovie: "Wetin yu de ask?"

Olamilekan: "As in, the details wey yu de find na for wetin? Because I no go release the contact on empty-tank."

Dr. Ovie: "See dis guy; so, how much?"

Olamilekan: "We go reason. Wait! No be yur house yu de go direct?"

Dr. Ovie: "Na house."

Olamilekan: "Abeg, help me drop off dis woman wey come see my daughter. Wait, make I call her, I hope say she neva go far."

Dr. Ovie: "She de married?"

Olamilekan: "The husband don late."

7:44 pm

Dr. Ovie: "God's work of creation continues with man. He has created man like Himself and charged him with authority to create, develop and improve mankind. Cutting edge scientific innovation like In Vitro Fertilization, stem cells technology, and even democracy, the least is endless; all for the betterment of humanity. God almighty is answering thousands of prayers through IVF, restoring a lot of bodies through stem cells technology. God is aware our faith as humans is trash, substandard and unreal, hence He gave nod to science to perform works mere believe and faith would have worked in three seconds or less."

Aniete: "Hmmm! You said too much to comprehend in one breath. I have this friend of mine in Abuja. She's been married for some years without any children. I think they should try this IVF and give offsprings a chance. I'm very glad I shared these moments with you; truly enlightening. One can easily feel you said your academic life was poor just to get the attention of a woman." Dr. Ovie laughs out loud.

Dr. Ovie: "I'm glad I could be a source of knowledge. Please once more, I beg you, would you join me out for lunch, maybe tomorrow, maybe whenever you feel the need to."

Aniete: "No I can't. I'm sorry. You're married. Go to your wife."

Dr. Ovie: "Damn you; don't remind me of my wife."

Aniete: "Why are you angry?"

Dr. Ovie: "You just rejected me. You just turned me down, two times."

Aniete: "You have a wife; go on and tell me what does that matter."

Dr. Ovie: "Yeah! Really, what does it matter that I have a wife? Does that make me less eligible to be happy?"

Aniete: "No! Not at all. Adultery is not a concept of law, it's in the realm of morality. It restrains it's torture in the space called conscience. I know your wife and she's a nice woman. Lastly, I won't tolerate my husband chasing after women like he doesn't have a wife. If you can define the true and undiluted meaning of wife, then you'll leave me alone and keep your body together for the one you swore openly to be with. Shameless you." There's a five minutes silence.

Dr. Ovie: "See I was just asking on behalf of my friend. I love my wife."

Aniete: "That's for you and your God alone to tell. I don't care."

Dr. Ovie: "Good night."

Aniete: "Good night." Aniete alighted and slammed the passengers seat door aggressively the window reverberated.

Dr. Ovie drove home upset and was talking alone in the car. 'Devil. This one na Ogbanje. Na im kill the im husband. Kill the poor guy. Very rude. See as e answer me straight. Maybe na lawyer, women lawyers na issue. Kno kno wan kill dem. Ola, yu be biggest fool. Because na you deceive me to reason dis woman. Ovie yu de mess-up, woman wey de on her own de manage her life na im you de eye. This Ovie yu be fool o! Okay why Ola no go drop am as e be say she fine for im eye? Shebi no be im daughter she come see? Na me mess up; henceforth mind your business and focus on your family leave people women alone.'

Chapter fourteen
Saturday 25 April, 2020
90 MINUTES

Preparations were well underway, and the recall of Udoka was a morale booster for the whole school. He was such an influential figure. At six feet tall with dark complexion, he was a captain to look up to and an intellect to behold. The Saturday of the games came upon them all like a thief in the night, as no amount of preparation is sufficient for a big game.

The simple rule of the host-ground is that the first match host is arrived at by a pool, while the subsequent matches are played on the turf of the victorious team, or whichever turf the victorious team chooses to play on. Host-ground rules, win-bonuses and some other regulations of such nature were put in place to encourage winnings in the tournament; winnings encourage competitiveness. NASFAT academy boys team were the next to face NEWLAND high school male football team nicknamed the 'Kings' for the second round of matches, of which two of the four grouped teams would advance to the elimination rounds of the tournament. The overall final four teams who make it through the group stages and through the elimination rounds would be representatives of the state in the under-20 male football division of the National games festival which is to be held in Edo state, Nigeria in a couple of weeks.

Accordingly, NASFAT academy chose to play the match on the turf of NEWLAND high school after defeating GSS Igondo in their first match of the fixtures.

Coming into the second match day, in group L was NASFAT academy on top spot with three points and four goals difference; GSS Ikoli with three points and one goal difference. Then NEWLAND high kings came third with zero points and minus one goal difference, then GSS Igondo is sitting on bottom of the table with zero points and minus four goals difference.

On the day, and mainly due to covid-19 restrictions, there were two games scheduled to be held in NEWLAND high school turf. The reason for the preference of the NEWLAND high turf named 'glory haven' was due to the standard nature of the pitch at one hundred and five, by sixty-eight meters and standard goal posts. It also was the only non-government funded institution that boasted of a ready to use V.A.R facility in the entire state.

The female match between NEWLAND high queens and Pace college, Ojodu went underway. Pace college situated at Ojodu came into the match-up with three point and two goals difference after beating Fountain Ladies FC, four goals, to two in their opening match of the group. It was opted to be the first game on the pitch because the turf's condition won't be as good as it would have been had the males played first.

The female referee blew the game to a start and the countdown began. The NEWLAND queens led by Eniola Atapa, 16, were high spirited going into the game, and having lost the first match to St. Bridget girls football team three goals to one, on the same turf didn't seem to disturb them. This was evident as they controlled most of the ball in the first half of the game but weren't clinical in their finishing in front of the opponent's six-yard box. At the stroke of halftime, the deadlock was broken. Number 6 shirt, Benedicta Dimka played a perfect long ball through the middle of the pitch which landed in front of number 7 shirt, Esther Rilwan and she fired past the Fountain Ladies FC goalkeeper for the first goal of the match. This was a confidence booster. The game then went into halftime. At the start of the second half, the visitors got to a blazing start and produced a goal which was ruled for offside leaving the score at one - nil to the hosts.

Midway into the second half, there were two substitutions from the host team to solidify the defense and try to hold on to the lead. Few minutes to the end of normal time, a brilliant play started by the number 2 shirt, Benedicta Dimka for the home side. A total of thirty-seven passes led to the second goal for the host side and the second goal for Esther Rilwan through an assist from number 6 shirt, Teni Ajunoh. There was general excitement in the school. From security-men at the gates, to janitors in the hostels, the entire school was joyous to receive their first win and with a clean-sheet. At the sound of the final whistle, the principal's excitement was written all over him as he couldn't hide his feelings, he's clapping forever. He loved the performance the young ladies displayed.

The celebration was short-lived as the referee in charge of the male division match-up started whistling. Soon after the male footballers started coming onto the field. The starting lineup is made up of eleven of the most experienced players available to the coaches. Virtually all boarding house students and probably every member of staff of the institution came out to watch the game disregarding the safety measures imposed by the government at different levels. The support of the entire school proved massive for the home players. They came out in a series of attacks and well organized plays during most of the first-half. At the thirty-third minute, the ball was moved from the center of the field on a counter attack with three defenders dashing back for cover. The NASFAT goalkeeper is watching his line. There are free and wide open spaces; the ball is passed back and forth between shirt number 7 and shirt number 8. Shirt number 8 continues advancing with the ball until a couple of yards before the penalty box, pulling the opposition team players to himself and then squares the ball across to shirt number 7 who holds the ball for two seconds and passes to shirt number 9 who fakes a shot but holds on to the ball, both visiting central defenders fell for the dummy and slide on the turf. The third defender hurried back to the goal line. Shirt number 7 dribbles in front of the goalie and fakes another shot, this time the goalie dives to his left and shirt number 7 hits the ball the opposite direction beyond the reach of the standing defender and the two who hadn't yet made it to their feet. It was a goal.

'Goal!' They all screamed. Shirt number 7, Jasper, ran ecstatic towards the bench, to his jubilant teammates and team managers. The visitors goalie remains in the turf burying his head to the ground. Shirt number 7 run fast with the other players following behind and dive into their fold and they all scream aloud. The team coach rubbed his head and waved them back onto the pitch. The visitors goalie took out the ball from the back of the net and kicked it to the opposite side of the pitch, gloomy looks appeared on his face and so was the look on the other players wearing the same jerseys on that pitch. On the sidelines, the cheerleaders are raising the momentum, they're raising and waving glamorous colors of pom-poms. Their energy was superb and heated up as they danced and cheered in colorful nose-masks.

The thrill of the match soon increased when the visiting team scored an equalizer at the forty-fourth minute.

The ball which was in possession of NEWLAND high kings shirt number 6, Andrew Bako, after a throw-in, then he passed a low-ball to shirt number 7, Jasper, both of them in the middle of the pitch and then shirt number 7 made a run right of the pitch and attempted a pass to shirt number 4, Malik Kando, the ball was intercepted by the opposition number 6, Roy Anakwe, who mis-tapped the ball back to the NEWLAND high kings number 7 who losses it again to the opposition shirt number 6 for the second time in one minute.

NASFAT Number 6 plays the ball wide and almost finds shirt number 8, Samuel Eneh, at the flank but loses the ball to a throw-in. Shirt number 3, James Aremu, of NEWLAND high kings took the throw-in and threw the ball deep into the penalty box of NASFAT academy which was held on by the goalkeeper. Immediately, the NASFAT goalie, Kabiru Inuwa released a long ball to the NASFAT shirt number 4, Silas Tanko who dashed forward on a counter attack towards the host half of the pitch. He had options; one was two players sprinting left, and a player opened up wide to the right. Shirt number 4 pushes forward a few more yards and plays a through ball to his left, to shirt number 10, Bashir Lawal, almost touching an opposition player on the way.

Shirt number 10 controls the ball with his left foot and loops it over the head of Obed, the host team's goalkeeper, for an equalizer and his fourth goal of the campaign. At one all, there was more to fight for.

"Defense! Defense!" Captain Udoka repeated several times after NASFAT academy equalized.

The mood in the stands didn't lower. Students and staff members cheered on. The principal was there present in the executive stand with a few guests of his. At halftime, the coaching crew gathered with the players in the dressing room.

Coach: "Brilliant performance boys, you soaked them up. We have to keep pushing and hopefully we'll get a few more goals. 2, play with 6 when you get the ball; 6, play wider, and don't forget to fall back to assist 3. 9, remain powerful there and disturb their Centre-defenders." The coach is clapping his hands, he's speaking audibly, raising their morale to ceiling heights. He added,

"We have forty-five minutes to put this matter to rest. Two more goals and we sit comfortably above them. Obed releases the ball quickly. Target Jasper and Jerome. Likely substitutes are 4 and 5 so we can lock the defense. So we need early goals; pass the ball in less than a second and create space. Gentlemen, make it happen."

Udoka made all of them lock their fists in the middle of the dressing room, then the coach stood and spoke, "To victory!" They all chanted and raised their hands up to the roof. They ran out of the tunnel to the cheering supporters. With the chilly breeze in position, it was the perfect start to a final forty-five minutes of football to decide the qualifying fate of the both teams.

NASFAT academy boys had most of the position in the first fifteen minutes of the new half but rarely any scare going forward; a couple of shirt-pulling and minimal cursing came to light. Ego and depletion of energy prompted outbursts. Two yellow cards shown for reckless tackle and for retaliation. Three substitutions are made and the game becomes more stylish and entertaining.

There's an instance in the seventy-third minute where the center referee's body interrupts an attack started off by the visiting team, then the ball falls to the host team's possession and going forward, they make good passes with the ball and score a second goal. The home team made the goal look so easy. It took an extra seven or eight minutes to restart the match after the goal was rejected by the visitors citing obstruction from the referee. The goal stood and the morale of the visitors depleted until two more chances were created and taken by the host team, to go on and win the fixture four goals to one. Goals from Jasper, Malik and Rotimi saw the hosts claim their first three points of the campaign. The principal stood all the while after the final whistle was blown. He was visibly amazed. The energy from the students and staff members was insane, that day could pass for 'world celebration day'. The principal sent word to the players that there wouldn't be any assembly that day as he requested that they all slept in time to recover fully for the final game of the group stage.

Vera was turf-side all through the game, she at one point coordinated routines for the cheerleaders and provided drinking water for them two times. Her focus was Udoka and her love for football.

7:23 pm
Vera: "I'm like, O my gosh! O my gosh! Don't score, don't score. I was screaming. I mean like; that Bashir guy is a top player, like every time he came close to our box I began to fret. Obed is a darling, I promised him 5k for his saves. That guy has to win best keeper..."
Udoka: "Wassup with Tinuke?"
Vera: "She's going for a final surgery on Wednesday..., or maybe Thursday; I'm not sure, I'll ask Aunty Yvone; I know she's had two surgeries already. I won't lie, you guys did me proud today, see the way Jasper hit that ball hard, I thought he wanted to injure somebody. I screamed, I threw my nose-mask away, I ran, I almost kicked the advertisement board..."
Udoka: "So when are we going to see her?"
Vera: "I don't know, maybe anytime. Why are you asking me about Tinuke?"

Udoka: "Why are you talking about other guys, didn't I play well, aren't you going to mention you saw me on that pitch too? And maybe, some commendation."
Vera: "Oh! So that's what this is about. Why didn't you allow me to finish first."
Udoka: "So I'll wait till all your sweet sweet words have finished on others."
Vera: "See your small head. So which amongst the mentioned am I with at this hour?" Udoka chuckles and hits her elbow with his.
Udoka: "Thanks!"
"You're welcome." She replied.

Chapter fifteen
Saturday 2nd May, 2020
NEWLAND high school, Surulere

The weather was favorable for football. The principal of NEWLAND high school held a meeting with the turf managers and gave instructions and encouragement to them, he charged them to make the turf worthy of commendation. The school intends to float a professional football team and the principal uses these qualifying matches to showcase the stands and the turf. He also met with members of the press and briefed them on preparations made to accommodate about one hundred and fifty spectators to the stand in compliance with covid-19 protocol and measures adopted to ensure safety distancing. Hand sanitizers were distributed to supporters at the entrance of the fifteen thousand mini-stadium.

One by one people started making their way to the stands, starting with the school's staff members and then parents and well-wishers of competing athletes.

2:23 pm

Aniete had spoken with Olamilekan early in the day concerning the final match day of games to be played by both the male and female teams of the school. Olamilekan had arrived about eleven minutes earlier. Aniete came with Emeka and Ejike to witness Udoka play.

They joined Olamilekan who was there on the invitation of Udoka. His daughter can't play due to injuries she suffered from an accidental fall. Four of them sat side-by-side on the stand behind the goal post. Olamilekan is used to sitting behind the goalkeeper to encourage his daughter when she's playing.

Aniete: "Did your friend tell you what happened?" Olamilekan smile,

Olamilekan: "Yes, he did. He was upset. He blames me for talking him into dropping you off."

Aniete: "It was gentlemanly to take me home, however, it was unnecessary to ask me out. He's married. Isn't that a problem?"

Olamilekan: "But you aren't."

Aniete: "My husband is dead."

Olamilekan: "That's the point, he's no more. The oath was for death to do you path. Upon the death of a spouse, the living spouse is free of the oath. Marriage is not for the dead. It's not even for the unhealthy, talk more of the dead."

Aniete: "And so, if I'm to consider a companion, would he now be married?"

Olamilekan: "No, he ought not to be. But in Ovie's case, he's as good as not married. They are strangers in his house. Wait! How do you know his wife?"

Aniete: "I lied. I wanted him to feel frightened that I could reveal."

Olamilekan: "He'll love it. He's been seeking a divorce."

Aniete: "Why, what's wrong?"

Olamilekan: "Nothing. But will you agree with me that some wives are trees rooted in the ground as soon as they secure a man in marriage? No more progression, just bearing children and nothing more." Aniete starts laughing. "Yes, it's true. It's because their mothers don't teach them to compete with men for power or economic edge; they teach them to compete with women for men, hence they mature and fight with women over men rather than fight with men for position."

Aniete: "Mr parable, what are you trying to say?"

Olamilekan: "Just cross the t and dot the i, because it's not from my mouth you'll hear the president farted."

Aniete: "Okay o! I will." she smiled.

At three o'clock in the afternoon the referee blew the whistle to get the match started between NEWLAND high queens and Fountain Ladies football club, Iyana Ipaja. The hosts go into the match with three points from a possible six after losing their opening match and picking a win in the second match of the competition.

A few of the supporters that made their way into the stadium did so with drums and sticks, and a few musical instruments which lightened the arena and boosted the player's morale. At the stroke of halftime it was drawn as none of the ladies could hardly ever get real momentum to ignite some wonderful play. And then the referee blew for halftime. The goalless first-half started building tension amongst the players, especially the home team.

At the start of the second half, tensions brewed and hard tackles started flying in. The cursing and aggression heightened.

At the seventieth minute, there was an incident of insensitive tackle by a visiting team member which led to the injury and substitution of shirt number 6, Teni Ajumoh and she was replaced by shirt number 17, Maureen Pebble. The free-kick was played deep into the six-yard box of the visitors and the ball was adjudged by the referee, to have hit the hand of shirt number 4, Munsurat Akinde of Fountain Ladies FC and the referee pointed at the spot for a penalty. There was drama as Fountain Ladies FC players surrounded the referee in protests. The agitation led to two visiting players yellow carded. There was double checking of the penalty awarded through V.A.R and the penalty stood. Esther Rilwan stepped up and converted the penalty from the spot for the first goal of the match.

There were wild celebrations everywhere. Aniete and Olamilekan, Emeka and Ejike, with their chilled cans of watermelon juice and bread-rolls were all in celebratory mood. There was excitement in the air.

The NEWLAND high queens went on to win the match, one goal to nothing. They defended their lead for the rest of the game. The victory lifted them second on the group log to six points behind St. Bridget who qualified top with nine points and earned them qualification to the second stage of the qualifying round and a step closer to the National games festival through the 'School football' division and a cash team-preparation prize money of one million Naira.

As is practice, the pitch was cleared and treated in preparation for the male teams, NEWLAND high kings and GSS Igondo. So the female team took their rejoicing to the dressing room. The host team came into the match with three of a possible six points from a convincing win in their second match day, whereas their opponent GSS Igondo, have zero points, of a possible six.

Aniete and her sons are in high hopes. She's hoping Udoka will have a good game to consolidate the success recorded by Emeka early in the month. Olamilekan is quiet.

As the players make their way to the pitch, the supporters pour out love and encouragement from the stands. Aniete and Emeka are screaming "Udoka! Udoka! Udoka!" Repeatedly. Joy was in large supply and this was evident.

From the sound of the whistle, Igondo boys started blazing, throwing long-balls into the opposite end of the turf, taking the game to the hosts. This pressure mounting paid off in the twelfth minute. It happened that shirt number 8, Japheth Adekoya of Igondo boys was making a run down the left-flank and dribbled past two defenders and still had the ball. Host's shirt number 2, Udoka then slid in with a dangerous tackle and brought down the visitor's shirt number 8. The referee blew for a free-kick and yellow-carded the aggressor. He got up after being briefly checked by the medical team and opted to take the free-kick. It was a few yards to the penalty area and he took a direct hit. He took it perfectly, the ball ricocheted off the crossbar, then it hit the back of the host's goalkeeper, Obed and right across the goal line and into the net. There was graveyard silence in the stadium. There were stoppages in heartbeats.

Udoka: "Move! Move! Move!" He yelled, then regrouped and continued play after light celebration from the visitors.

At the thirty-third minute, Udoka moved on to a free space he found from the left after a handball was spotted by the assistant referee. Malik passed the ball to Udoka who made a sprint to the center of the field from the left rear-end of the field and moved forward as the Igondo boys kept on withdrawing, anticipating a pass. He got close and opted for a shot at goal. The strike was well hit, the ball deflected off a visitor's body and on for a corner. Jasper took the corner-kick and the ball landed comfortably on the head of Udoka who hit it hard to the far corner beyond the head and gloves of the visitors. Unsurprisingly, after the header, Udoka ran to the goal post and collected the ball, held it back to the center of the field and placed it on the ground.

Udoka: "Move! Move! Move!" He was lifting everybody.

The game continues and as expected, the aggressive nature of males reveals itself.

Olamilekan: "At one goal a piece, it is comfortable for us, we have four points as it stands, because news reaching us is that Ikoli is defeating NASFAT currently. And if it stays like that, and this match ends like this, then we'll qualify with four points. An outright win here will be better. Qualification hangs on the outcome of the match between NASFAT academy and GSS Ikoli."

Aniete: "My heart is beating fast." Olamilekan laugh,

Olamilekan: "Don't worry, you'll be fine. By the way, congratulations on his goal. Great step in the right direction."

Aniete: "Thank you! Thank you! Their father is looking down on them." Olamilekan chuckles.

Olamilekan: "You know, your opinion about my friend, Ovie, is not surprising to me because humans talk momentously; they speak based on how they feel, driven by a particular emotion. Or perhaps, different emotions. And then when another feeling, or emotion change occurs, because emotional change must occur, and therefore affect their feelings and their position or stupid argument has changed, you'll notice pride and ego won't make them go back to where they were publicly saying rubbish and apologize. They'll say 'E don pass' am I lying?"

Aniete: "I don't understand!"

Olamilekan: "Don't worry."

Aniete: "Make me understand what you're saying. Look, time spent, no matter how short the moment was, it's still a stretch of time and must have its space in memory's shelf. I had a good moment with your friend. I like the fact we went to the same school, but I don't also want to admire another woman's possession. If it's true they are having issues in their home, they better resolve it. They don't know what they have until they have to live without it. You're married for some time so I believe you understand there's no perfect home or marriage. There's at best near-perfect spouses putting in work together trying to make a good home and a marriage worthy of these unfortunate times marriages find themselves in."

Olamilekan: "I hear you."

The match ended at two all. Igondo boys scored a second goal in the second-half and the host replied with a goal from shirt number 7, Jasper through an assist by shirt number 2, Udoka. The final whistle ensured that NEWLAND high school finished second on the log behind GSS Ikoli who collected all nine points with three wins. NASFAT and Igondo finished third and fourth respectively.

Due to regulations on social distancing, the principal opted for a quiet celebration. He addressed an assembly a few hours after the game and expressed confidence in the athletic abilities of the female and male football teams as well as students competing in the other forms of sporting events. He gave athletes and students each a cash prize of fifty thousand Naira. The students number about one hundred and thirteen.

Principal: "Congratulations to you all, keep soaring high in all your endeavors. Make yourselves proud, make your family proud, make your community proud, make your country proud. I love you all and may God almighty be with you all."

Chapter sixteen
Meanwhile

During their transit within time from 2020 back to the fourteenth century, earth's magnetic fields, tidal forces of the sun and moon, solar flares contributed to some difficulty the travelers encountered on their quest to save modern Africa by correcting yesterday. Darkspirits, hellspirits, guardian and freespirits ferried the news of a trip back in time to their respective covens and shelters.

Activities of such magnitude don't occur often. There are processes and lobbying mandatory for permission to return earth to a position where it was while rotating and revolving in motions-past; there is utter need for master precision and utmost care in initiating and executing such missions. Many who have attempted a trip to time-past after necessary checks and balances have not returned. Over the centuries, truths available show that many people who did travel back in time arrived, but there was a problem returning to the present time from when they went back in time. The issue mostly reported was a majority of them do not understand the translation or technique to activate the enchanting words and patterns in the new era they arrived at. Others arrived at unpleasant places and savagery times where they were eaten by their hosts. Some others, it was reported, just refused to come back to present time.

The transit entails total and thorough reduction of the body parts to the smallest particles of soil- a core component of nature and begin to spin off the ground like a tornado and suspend in the clouds. The pace of the whirling of the traveler in soil-form determines the extent of the year he's returning to. The process is the body parts reduce into the smallest molecules of matter just like fine dust, then these small particles of the traveler whirling anti-clockwise initially with lazy progressive motion would then increase up to a speed of sound, ascend and suspend in clouds in a process called Mpkosa, and upon arrival at the destination of the time-traveler, fine particles of sand come together like metal to magnet and form a body for the spirit of the traveler to dwell. Hafeez arrived first due to his size. He arrived about eight minutes before Tinuke. Upon his appearance on the soil, his small particles attracted like a magnet and pieced together. Asleep, he was held by the guards that responded to screaming for help by the locals in the presence of a strange sighting. There he was locked up in a cage-like cell made of acacia trees fitted by specially carved bolts, exposed publicly like they display caged rare wild animals captured in the wild or captured desert beasts for the viewing pleasure of Malian citizens. At this time, their supreme rulers led by the Mansa of Mali kingdom had embarked on a journey to the holy city, so the ultimate mandate of leadership of the Mali empire was on eighteen years old Torro. A direct kin to the pilgrimaging ruler. It was his decision to detain Hafeez, a strange being until the priests who didn't accompany the ruler to the holy city arrived. Hafeez was terrified when he woke up, visibly frightened. The air was thick-hot, the stench was moist wood, pepper and dust. On the arrival of the priest, Achunaki, who rolled twenty deep rode on a white horse; while all other warriors in his fleet rode on black horses adorned with gold on their ears, on some noses, necks, wrists, ankles and as well on the horses; they sparkled, carrying spears, swords and bronze made shields. Only then was the boy ordered to be clothed and taken out of the cage where he was paraded. However, his hands were mildly bound, same as his feet.

Shortly after, there was a wave with strong whirling winds. Mighty breeze caused specs of sand to disobey gravitational force and blew it then raised thick dust from the ground making sight difficult. And then as the dust settled, there was a young woman on the ground. Tinuke laid on the soil, undressed. Regardless of the dust that she was covered in, all the yelling around her, she was sound asleep.

Tinuke woke up to the sound of Hafeez screaming. The sun shined upon her violently her eye-lid would not rollback so she could barely see; dust again began rising and sinking into her nostrils, soaking her hair, caused majorly by aggressive beatings on the dry ground by large sized feet laced to knee level by sandals made of threads, buckles and leather soles worn by special guards called in to confront the mysterious visitors. And there she was wrapped up in the sand surrounded and threatened by dwarfs brandishing spears and shields carved out of steel with ivory and gold holders, pointing at her and attempting to poke her; ten, maybe fifteen of them humming in unison. It's scorching hot and the orange skies were impossible to stare at. Yet the sound of Hafeez pierced through to her heart and she responded, even though struggling with getting off the ground "Hafeez, I'm coming to get you!" repeatedly.

The arrival of Tinuke caused apprehension and mild panic generally amongst the locals. They were already making up stories about the sudden emergence of a little boy and then another gender arrived out of choreographed dust. Achunaki ordered that she be taken to the female ward and dressed up by the female wardens. She resisted vehemently several attempts to seize her, this caused injuries on her body. The metal on their fingers, the rings and bracelets worn by the guards tore her skin and it caused her great pain. Regardless, fearless Tinuke resisted them. She requested to see Hafeez but due to language barrier they couldn't communicate. The dominantly Mende speaking people didn't understand what Tinuke and Hafeez were saying. From a distance, Hafeez screamed even louder; his voice echoed, he was afraid also. Tinuke heard the trembling in his voice. But in reality they were just a couple of meters apart from each other in separate room-cells made of mud brick and roofed with timber and reed with tiny holes dug in the walls for lightning and ventilation after Tinuke was returned from the female ward being clothed in a black garment, sandals strapped to her knees and a matching scarf long enough for a wrapper to cover up her hair. They were taken there in order not to contaminate the citizens as they perceived the visitors were unbelievers.

Around night time when their energy had depleted they had stopped screaming, they were quiet and humble. To their greatest surprise there was adequate lighting of the small city called Maroja, which means, place of keep or prison yard in the tribe of Mende.

Two bowls of hot millet porridge with honey and chicken wings were served and they both ate convincingly as they were famished for food and rest. Shortly after the meal Hafeez reported stomach hurting and he threw up all he had consumed. Tinuke was trying to signal that Hafeez needs a doctor, but the warrior dwarfs of the special forces who guarded them didn't utter any words nor did they even blink on them one second; they were simply humming.

He was later removed from the cell and taken to the lodge of the priest, Achunaki. At this point Hafeez became cold for his body had been exposed the whole while. Time-travel cannot accommodate any matter outside the human body, no clothing accompanied them. On the orders of Adolia, Hafeez was wrapped in white linen cloth and put in a room in the upper section of the lodge where there was a lit up fireplace. Special spices were mixed in herbal liquid and robbed all over his body, his fingers and toenails were painted white. He was forced to drink some herbal medicine and then he began sweating profusely; his headache when the mud-brick walls around him were spinning; he threw up a few times, he cried until he slept off.

Moments after Achunaki returns to the room-cells alone also dressed in white Yemeni silk sewn in one piece from top to bottom; he had a red turban on his head and black beads rolled around his wrist. Then on his left shoulder was a raven which was flapping its wings rumpling the red turban on his head. The guards manning the cells let him into Tinuke's cell and the sight of him in the deep of night frightened her as she withdrew from the door of the cell. She was panting heavily. "We want to see Mansa!" Tinuke said. Hafeez' room-cell was quiet because he had been taken away. The pilot raven struggling to balance now on the left arm of Achunaki croaked aggressively at Tinuke and she repeatedly screamed; her back to the opposite end of the mud-brick wall of the room-cell, "We want to see the Mansa!" Achunaki immediately withdraws from the entrance of the cell and releases the raven which flies through different corners of the structure housing the cells and flies out to the open. On the rooftop of the two-storey mud-brick structure were many more ravens which accompanied the pilot raven. Together they flew at speeds beyond telling, croaking without cease. Over hills, palm trees, valleys and massive desert lands they paced; each holding a position from start until they arrived at the voyage of the Mansa of Mali empire and on his howdah the pilot raven perched. Two of the accompanying ravens perched on the howdah of the chief priest leading the priests accompanying the voyage; his howdah always preceded the procession of more than one thousand pilgrimaging Malians. At once the camels whereupon the howdah is placed halted and the chief priest alighted with the help of three servants. The warriors guarding his howdah on black horses halted as well, followed by many others. These mean-faced warriors as well as others, each had a golden Mansa medallion looking like midgets hanging on their necks with carved gold pendant masks.

Mali Empire
1324 A.D

Huarhkim: "Where is the boy? I can't seem to see him clearly, I see many boys his size but his face eludes me; perhaps I get close to the girl and learn about his whereabouts."

Aliliga: "Your excellency, the boy was last taken to the abode of the priest, Achunaki. Word hasn't been heard from him since. Earspirits tell his stay here is limited, but only after he's fulfilled his mission can he leave."

Huarhkim: "Tell me more!"

Aliliga: "His task is to dissuade the Mansa from announcing wealth of a people whose weakness forbid them from protecting such treasures. The consequences for which they suffer six hundred years after due to sustained schematic conflicts for these precious stones. Word have reached the Mansa about the arrival of visitors from the future."

Huarhkim: "I have to draw closer to the girl; I have to cease this moment and leave with the same powerful magic with which they came. I need the boy's body; I need new skin. This body sucks, it is tired and unattractive. I need the boy's body. Behold at the point of exit from this era I shall intercept the boy's astroperson, displace the his spirit and I shall possess his new and shiny body."

Aliliga: "Very well your excellency, I'll arrange a meeting with her at once. One more thing, your excellency, higher earspirits report the presence of darkspirits as well as more hellspirits in this community. They claim air theses presence of spirits of different covens and shelters increased when the girl and the boy arrived, hence, your excellency you must be swift for demand is higher than supply."

Huarhkim: "I shall."

At that time, Achunaki had in his household tens of servants and those students he taught the laws and the books. There was a maidservant, Velus, who was bought from Arabian slave merchants and positioned to cater for Adolia, Achunaki's oldest wife. Velus was fond of Tinuke, and often made way undisturbed to her room-cell with special dishes and tales about Hafeez who was in the keep of Achunaki.

And on the fifteenth day of their arrival, when she came to serve food for Tinuke, Velus was dressed in a gown made of brocade and Yemeni silk on leather sandals and matching burqa. They discussed and shared deep and strong emotions.

Tinuke: "Friend please I need your help!" Startled, Velus asked, "How do you speak our dialect, and very well pronounced words?" "I listened!" Tinuke replied.

Velus: "Wow! That's great. I'm Velus, from the tribe of Ayikati, I was captured in my village faraway from here when I was a little girl and we were brought here by men who get paid by slave merchants to kidnap young men, women and children. It took me almost a lifetime to speak, however I understood their dialect not long after I was brought here, but it took me longer than you for sure. Now that you can hear and speak our mother-tongue, let's discuss. Who are you and what are you doing here and is that boy your son?"

Tinuke: "I'm Tinuke Ajose, I'm from the Yoruba tribe in Nigeria. I'm from the future. That boy, Hafeez is my brother and he was chosen along with many other children by a beautiful queen, Idia, for us to spread and reawaken the black-race consciousness which has been wiped off the history books by whites who came as friends but ended up as snakes."

Velus: "I don't understand. How come a queen will send you on an errand without clothing for you? The story is that you were found naked."

Tinuke: "The nature of this mission we've embarked upon consists mainly of us traveling to time past and spreading a new message that will better shape the tomorrow or blacks across the world."

Velus: "I don't understand..."

Tinuke: "Let me finish. When you travel through a portal back in time, the body does not go as a whole, it must be reduced to fine particles of soil or sand and through fast spinning winds like a mini-tornado, the traveler is conveyed by magical powers to the destination and time he's traveling; the spinning causes the drowsiness."

Velus: "This portal you speak, how can I access it or how do I access it?"

Tinuke: "You don't need it, unless you want to travel to a different era which is nearly impossible as there are layers of security checks to prevent miscreants from tampering with nature's order of events."

Velus: "But I'd love to adventure to another time and place, maybe travel back home. Hold on a minute, how do you know this much? you're just about my age."

Tinuke: "You're right; I didn't know much about myself other than football. We were taught by the powerful queen how to use words and signs to travel. How to guard and defend the messenger and finally how to return when the skies turn brown; that's how we know our time is up."

They spoke at length being girls of similar age-bracket. Velus was very much interested in the future. She wanted to know the fate of her family, her home and community.

Velus: "When you get back can you help me seek from the powerful queen the nature and wellbeing of my people. Since I was taken into slavery I only think about where everyone is, how everyone is. I wear a smile on my face to help me cover the pain; I'm always holding back tears. When I cater and care for my lady Adolia, I wish someone was taking care of my mother." Sobering, she adds, "Do you have a mother?"

"Yes, I do," Tinuke replied. "I can't wait to get back to the house to see her. If we don't return, or if I don't return with Hafeez, I'm afraid something might go wrong with her. She loves and adores Hafeez like her only child." She added.

It was uncomfortably hot city-wide and this made Tinuke more upset that she wouldn't eat yam porridge and yogurt Velus served.

Velus: "When are you going to see Mansa? From my calculations it will take up to four or five months to meet up with the camel-train. I heard from my lady Adolia that word has been sent to the Mansa about your arrival, but that the courier ravens haven't returned. My master Achunaki has been sleepless now. He sees nothing relating to you both; but he awaits instructions from his superiors who are pilgrimaging with the Mansa."

Tinuke: "Sleepless nights? Why is that?"

Velus: "Guardians of the empire believe your presence has awakened higher dimension spirits who would wish to access the channel used by you both to exit this era. Therefore they are at premium alert, watching against any invasion."

Tinuke: "Please, how do I get out of here, I have to fasten the process of this mission and return Hafeez home. I need your help."

Velus: "I feel your plight, I know firsthand how it feels when you're taken away from your home, family and away from love to a place where none exist. What do you want?"

Tinuke: "I want a lot of things to happen fast; I wish for time to stop. There's many things needing to be done and more on the way. I fear if time isn't paused there will be more things piling up and may remain undone."

Velus: "We need a plan!"

At night time of the fifteenth day of the first month of their arrival, the pilot raven had returned to the empire with news from the chief priest.

Achunaki: "The elders have spoken, words have returned from the howdah of our kingdom. Mansa wants to meet with them personally when he returns from his pilgrimage. Therefore, we must keep them longer here and wait for the powers who sent them to our era to come collect them. We cannot afford to fold our arms and allow these spies to learn about our defense system then lead an enemy army against us. We must therefore prescribe the penalty deserving for treachery; death. Their arrival is causing me to panic. Their uninvited arrival is causing our empire tensions."

Achunaki was addressing an assembly of elders of the communities of the empire led by Torro.

At midnight of the morning of the sixteenth day, there were strange natural occurrences throughout the sweltered small city of Maroja. First, rain began drizzling, then the water evaporated, the vapor compacted the entire community and visibility became poor. The guardsmen, upon instructions given to them by Achunaki, through trumpet blasting signaled the citizens of Maroja of a security threat and that all should be in combat mode. This vapor would settle moments after and though night, the moon gave sound vision for the eyes. Then tiny flaming rocks started raining from the skies like air-to-ground missiles; it was raining rocks.

114

This caused tension in the whole place as citizens scampered for safety at the dead of night; horses broke open barn doors, the camels and other animals ran off. The rocks melted any substance it landed on, tore open mud-brick walls. Flaming rocks traveling at many miles per hour burnt out timber and reed made roofs, animals hide and human skin. Then the raining flaming rocks cease dropping from the skies and then followed by another session of drizzling rain which extinguished the burning palm trees, houses, clothes and dry grasses. More vapor compacted the place. Breathing was difficult, the aged men and women were at risk as they all grappled with lack of oxygen.

The night stretched into other nights as morning light refused to come on. And then eventually daylight appeared and the assault on man by nature ceased. There was a general headcount to ascertain the number of survivors and this exercise revealed that thirty-three citizens and servants died in total. Torro was sad, he accused Tinuke and Hafeez of coming from hell and causing the wreckage in their city. He ordered them to be beheaded and their bodies cast out in the desert of Zuni. Achunaki warned him that the best thing to do was to send them to see the Mansa and so accomplish their mission so they can return to where they came from instead of taking their lives here which could further endanger their entire lives.

Torro: "Is it not that the Mansa conveyed to us that he would not meet with any guests until his return?"

Achunaki: "Yes, that is correct my lord, however, owing to such occurrences like we witnessed, we cannot afford to keep them here much longer. Prophetic words report that high dimension spirits are interested in them as it has been confirmed that they indeed came from the future as they claim. Darkspirits, freespirits and hellspirits are interested in them or something about them. We must set them to depart to meet with the Mansa."

Torro: "But how can that be? The procession is about four months so far; or at least they must have been gone four or five months into the trip. How do we take them there?"

Achunaki: "My lord, we shall take them with the aid of the Queen bird."

Torro: "The Queen bird?"

Achunaki: "My lord we're left with no choice. If you may, my lord, grant that one shall go and one shall stay, we cannot have them both go in other that we avert any harm upon the two of them. We shall transport the girl

first and hold the boy. Her message will be more convincing than those of the little boy."
Torro: "Granted!"

At midnight of the morning of the seventeenth day, the small city of Moraja witnesses yet another day to remember. Achunaki led some guards east of the city and arrived at a field of vast green grasses and thousands of Palm trees; the guards holding lanterns and cans of oil. This was considered the most sacred place in the entire kingdom because of the presence of incomprehensible creatures which lived and protected the citizens for centuries. Upon arrival on horses at the foot of the vast fields of green grasses, the guards put off their lanterns and started drumming and humming rhythmically. Achunaki alighted, slowly taking quiet steps inward the fields of vast green grasses, he started chanting and singing hymns aloud, he danced to the sound of the drummers and there in the thick of darkness a loud croak was heard, the sound echoed miles away, Achunaki and the guards trembled. The horses didn't run off. It was the Queen bird, the mother Raven, at more than 1.70 meters in height, body is larger than a mini-truck; the creature walked out of darkness and approached the men. In majesty she strolled towards them, her claws crushing earth like excavators, tarsus wider than truck tyre, moonlight reflecting on the glossy feathers. Her wings larger than pool tables, her eyes and approaching lower and upper beaks paused heartbeat; she was enormous. No other way around for taking the visitors to meet with the Mansa as it was a matter that called for sound-speed travel to see the Mansa who had already embarked upon a trip so that the task of 'fore-warning' will the accomplished and thus the gateway to returning to the era- the modern era from which they came would be opened. The citizens of the kingdom were living in fears and concern over the appearance and stay of two visitors whose presence is causing mysterious things to happen. Whose presence has attracted spirits of multiple shelters to dwell in the kingdom and seek ways around them due to the mighty powers that accompany them and surround them.
She croaked severally and began flapping her jet-size wings blowing breeze everywhere the Palm trees and other trees are dancing, Achunaki and the men, along with the grazing horses were tossed around and staggered for balance.

Tinuke was persuaded by Velus, Achunaki's oldest wife's maidservant to take a drink made of herbs and sedatives so as to endure the flight to meet with the pilgrimaging Mansa, which she did without hesitating. Before a few minutes went by, she fell deep asleep and was taken by the cell-guards, closely followed by Velus and other maidservants to the passage, a hilltop where she'll be left for the queen bird to pick up. Trips like this, where the ability of the Queen bird or mother raven were always reserved for night time because of the frightening size of the bird. Many citizens and members of the kingdom have heard about the fields of vast green grasses and about the incomprehensible species of animals that are resident there. However in this case, many who were awake witnessed the landing of the mother raven, the croak was audacious.

Carefully lifting Tinuke into her lower beak, the mother raven departed and flew the same distance the pilot ravens had flew; this time around a lot quicker.

Three days later, after traveling hundreds of miles, the mother raven arrived at the convoy of the Mansa. Hundreds of men started drumming and humming; then there the chief priest accompanying the voyage greeted the queen bird with rhythmic dance steps and humming, quite similar to Achunaki's. She was deposited on the sandy soil asleep, where slimy substance wrapped her body; adhesive, soft and moisturizing substances glued sand on her and the warriors protecting the procession lifted her, cleaned and got her ready to meet with their supreme leader. This was night time and the camps of men, women and slaves were resting for the day.

The camp of the Mansa, supreme leader of the Malians along with several top pilgrimaging citizens was several meters away from the rest of the traveling Malians. The chief priest, dressed in white Persian silk thobe with white matching turban and black ghutrah took sleepy Tinuke by her hand in his right hand and a lantern in his left hand and led her to the tent of the Mansa, accompanied by twelve praying priests. These priests primarily teach the laws and holy book to the citizens and subjects in schools and in prayer places.

Chief priest: "Your highness, here is your guest."

Mansa: "Come!" Tinuke went ahead to meet him while the rest of the people stayed at the foot of his tent. A quavering Tinuke took slow steps toward him as he backed the entrance of the tent signaling his unwillingness to entertain any guests. As she arrived, she fell on her knees and sobbing she said, "Good morning your highness. I am Tinuke Ajose and I came from a long distance to meet with you." As she spoke, the chief priest and other praying priests stood paying attention to details she uttered, while humming In unison.

Mansa: "Speak!"

Tinuke: "The spirit of Queen Idia, queen of Benin kingdom in modern day Nigeria greets you, she lived and died two hundred years after you in the future to be, and has assembled us to go and tell the new truth about modern day Africa."

Mansa: "What is Africa, and why is this queen interested in me? I have many wives and girlfriends; perhaps she thinks I'll live to meet with her." He smiles, there's relief in Tinuke who smiles as well. "Your highness," Tinuke said, "Africa is a great space where people of dark skin majorly reside. The area where your kingdom is situated and larger areas make up Africa. And the queen, she is not interested in being your queen, but is interested in the emancipation of modern African children."

Mansa: "Why did she send you to me? What role do I have to play in liberating people I do not govern? They must have a leader who is saddled with the task of breaking the chain of bondage around the necks of his people."

Tinuke: "That is exactly why we came, the era we find ourselves in is completely complicated as white men came and took our resources away, burned down our sites and holy places of worship, killed our leaders and took as slaves our young people. They in-turn instill hatred and division among the people so they do not unify, progress or develop to be prosperous."

Mansa: "What do I do to help a situation that will occur after my death?"

Tinuke: "Do not announce Africa. Do not display such wealth as you intend, these whites will attack your people and black peoples in years to come because we do not possess the sophisticated army and weaponry needed to protect our lives and resources."

Mansa: "Your queen sent you to blame me for being wealthy and greatly generous?"

118

Tinuke: "Not quite, your highness, there are series of events that led to different peoples at different times meeting with different white guests and ceding control over territories to those snakes who pretended to be noble and honest."

Mansa: "So you accuse me of allowing snakes to infiltrate our kingdoms hundreds of years after?"

Chief priest: "What great power surrounds you? I can't seem to see beyond your body's surface, your eyes elude me as well." "Ancestral magical powers brought us here and sustain us. Our yesterday hangs on a balance of events pending his highness' actions we have come to alter or prevent. If you don't go about what you're doing the way you're doing many of our modern era realities would be different for the better."

Mansa: "Where is the boy?"

Tinuke: "He's held at the lodge of Achunaki, he is in good health, he's only afraid of what is to come."

Mansa: "Take her away! Get me the boy." At once Tinuke was seized by the hand and pulled out of the tent of the Mansa. She's screaming, refusing to be removed from his presence, "Thanks to you, they came in search of precious metals. They came lying that they're friends and preyed on our ancestors. Armed with evil thoughts, they rewrote history and painted us as parasites. We cannot continue to watch them take what is ours, we're only asking for what was stolen from us for hundreds of years. The evil guests we hosted backed by their criminal governments have done enough harm. We've had enough of their narratives." She was pulled to a tent where she was watched over until the following night to be reconvened to the city of Maroja by yet another great flight. There at the tent, Tinuke was given beans and chicken, milk, and honey for her meal but she refused everything.

Four days later through yet another great flight, Hafeez was presented to the Mansa.

Chief priest: "Welcome friend! Thank you for joining us."

Hafeez: "Hello! Are you Musa?"

Chief priest: "Little man, we'd rather have you address him as 'Your highness'"

Hafeez: "That's okay. So when am I meeting with him?"

Chief priest: "As soon as possible." He smiles, and Hafeez smiles too. As they proceed to meet with the Mansa, the chief priest and Hafeez, they walk past many caravans of camels carrying tons of gold-bars and gold carved ornaments. Hundreds of black desert snakes with gold rings pierced into their tails covered in large empty barrels for a display of culture and cohabitation in terrifying beauty of glistening intermingling stones. There were men adorned in gold, from ears, to necks, to noses, to bellies, to wrists, ankles and toes; gold everywhere on the bodies of thousands of men who were on pilgrimage from their kingdom to the holy city ably led by their supreme leader. Hundreds of horses carrying food supplies for years of journeying. Highly paid Berbers rolling fifty-deep escorting the caravans. Everyone was gathering to look at him, some even touched him; young and old people alike. There were lots of privileges and mysteries surrounding him, Hafeez- the great flight, the trip from the future, the privilege of meeting and dining with the Mansa, the audience of the ruling class. Hafeez was an instant star. His outfit was Royal, leather sandals with gold buckles, laced up to knee level. Black armless robe with s golden medallion of the image of the Mansa hanging like a midget in his little neck. His head was wrapped by black and white checkered ghutrah.

They arrived at the entrance of the tent of the Mansa and the chief priest knelt down and bowed, while Hafeez stood.

Chief priest: "Your highness, the boy you requested." Bowing his head he left the tent. Hafeez took tiny steps and advanced the stool of Mali where the Mansa sat, the symbol of supremacy, power and control over all of Mali empire. He sat backing the entrance door.

Hafeez: "Your highness, why did you ask the bird to carry me? Nobody asked if I wanted to be ferried by a big bird." Looking surprised, needing answers. "It swallowed me, put very cold slimy stinky saliva all over me; I couldn't see, I couldn't breathe, I cried and cried and now I'm cold."
Mansa: "I ordered that you be spiced and wrapped up during your trip so you stay warm in the bosom of the mother raven."
Chief priest: "He wouldn't drink the sedative herbs."
Hafeez: "And that's how they were dragging and humiliating me and Tinuke. There was no regard for diplomatic relations. I ate food and felt ill because of the flies perpetually perching on everything my eyes could see. And those dwarfs injured Tinuke's hand and her body. We were crying, they didn't bother, threatening to pierce our bodies with sharp swords and spears. Say sorry. Okay say something, anything." he was

visibly upset. "I was put in a cage and paraded for everyone to gaze at like a common criminal." He added.

"I thought you brought the girl to me because this one couldn't speak?" Mansa said, "Adolia taught him." The chief priest replied.

Mansa: "Little man, are you really a child? Where are you from? What do you seek that brings you to my kingdom?" Hafeez is sitting on the Persian rug in the tent. Milk and yam porridge is served next to him, the trays of food are placed on small ivory carved tray-holders in between him and the Mansa sitting on an elevated gold carved stool; flies are perching on the food, Hafeez is waving his hands over the trays, protecting the meals from the flies.

Hafeez: "If you aren't ready to eat, make them cover it, see flies all over it."

Mansa: "Oh! Apologies little friend, the food is for your tummy's fill."

Hafeez: "I'm Hafeez, I'm not a little man, I'm a big boy and I'm definitely not eating that." Mansa signaled with his left index finger, waving it sideways; then a young female servant who was always on standby entered the tent and removed the trays holding the variety of meals and drinks.

Mansa: "Hafeez, I like your name; what does it mean?"

Hafeez: "I don't know; okay I know but I don't remember. When I get back home I'll ask my mummy."

Mansa: "The queen is your mother?"

Hafeez: "No! My mummy is young and beautiful. Mrs. Ajose is her name."

Mansa: "If the queen is not your mother, then who is the queen? And why would your mother let a little child like you out of her sight, Hafeez."

Hafeez: "I just know she's a queen and everyone bows to greet her; I mean everyone. And my mummy doesn't know I'm here. Queen Idia told us not to tell our parents; she said they'll refuse."

Mansa: "The queen told you not to seek consent from your mother. That queen is a witch."

Hafeez: "She's not. She's kind and she loves humanity, that's why you can see she's assembling young children to correct anomalies of the past, such as this."

Mansa: "Are you really a child? You amaze me what you say, more than you can speak and understand our dialect. I've never seen stranger days.

121

Tell me, does the queen want to be my bride? I marvel at her insistence on me. Or is she solely interested in my wealth?" Hafeez is laughing. "Marry you?" He touted. She's married to Ozolua!" He added. "Let me tell you, seven hundred years from now, Africa is in a terrible state of affairs. Her governments are against her people. Her governors join hands with foreigners to steal her resources and enrich themselves, stash large sums of money abroad and willfully under-develop the entire continent. The citizens of Africa die daily by the strategic and continuous wicked actions and omissions of their leaders. Their leader's allegiances belong to strangers because of the largesse they collect to betray and dehumanize their kinsmen..."

Mansa: "Largesse!"

Hafeez: "...and women." Hafeez chortles,

Mansa: "I like that word. Largesse! You're intelligent..." Hafeez chuckles, and says, "More like, I'm one of a kind!" They both smile at each other.

Mansa: "But what has all of these got to do with me?"

Hafeez: "Exactly! It has everything to do with you and a couple other African rulers of old. When a boy buys candies he keeps them safe..."

Mansa: "What are candies?"

Hafeez: "Candies means more than one candy."

Mansa: "Oh! Okay."

Hafeez: "Now, when he buys them and a few biscuits, he protects them so other children can't steal them; he puts them in his pockets or in his school bags. But when he doesn't have pockets, maybe he's wearing his pajamas he can lose his candies and biscuits. Now Africa has all these golds and diamonds and oils and everything but she doesn't know how to protect them and preserve them for us and our unborn children so theses white peoples because of their guns and rockets and jets and everything they've got they come and steal and degrade the places, they don't cater for the soil, the fish in the water, the wellbeing of the grannies. They don't care about us. They just take take and take and leave pain and destruction behind. Wars for precious metals and crude oil have torn Africa apart. Our gift has become our curse. Your highness, when you take these many stones to show these people, you're inviting them to know if more exist. It's happening In a time when Africa does not have military wares to protect them. Why don't you consider improving your defense rather than announcing prematurely what you possess that you cannot protect. The remote effects are the millions of children and women displaced by disputes arising from trade in blood-diamonds, blood-gold, blood-oil." At this instant, there's increased air movement; the whole place where the pilgrims camped for the night became windy. Dry fine particles of dust rising from the ground, blocking nostrils even with face coverings.

Mansa: "Who told you all these?"

Hafeez: "My mummy, my daddy and the queen mother."

Mansa: "How can this be? My people are warriors."

Hafeez: "Wars have gone beyond swords and spears, your highness. They came with guns and subjected our people to treatments undeserving to animals. If you were in our times, you'll be arrested and prosecuted by animal rights activists for animal cruelty. All these weight on theses animals can cause permanent damage to their spines and invariably shorten their lifespan." The man crosses his legs, spreads out his purple flowing robe and folds his arm.

Mansa: "Your era amaze me, I thought it was the animal's destiny to delight his owner; I thought it was the place of the animal to serve and feed the man, and not the other way round. I'd love to visit your time and experience all these words you tell."

Hafeez: "You can't come, we don't wear these kinds of sandals anymore."

Mansa: "Now I'm convinced you're not a child. Or perhaps you've been overshadowed by the witch queen. How can you know all these things and all the times and not be a witch? You ought to be put to death for the spirit you possess ought not be allowed to continue with these false gospels. You lie against people, you accuse them of evil acts, you call royalties thieves, you accuse governments of crimes and attacks against the black race, all these to occur in the future. You claim to have knowledge of tomorrow. Now tell me, did I successfully make it to the holy city, and what lies the fate of my kingdom? Speak, or I have you thrown in the barrels of snakes." Hafeez trembles, he stutters, his heartbeat pauses.

Hafeez: "Your highness, you made even more success; you crashed the price of gold everywhere you went, your generosity to the poor ensures you are remembered in history as perhaps the richest and most charitable man of all time. You made it to the famous Catalan Atlas decades after your return." Mansa smiles and says, "May the will of God be done."

Hafeez: "Your opulence guided foreigners, especially Europeans to come in and grab more than all their imaginations created. Timbuktu will be invaded, the TRANS-Sahara Trade routes will be taken over, independent African states will be consumed by endless wars over control of natural resources all because of actions and omissions of African leaders of old. Their gunfire is much more superior to your golden spears and swords; their guided-missiles are more accurate and destructive than your arrows and thus, in the end your empire crumbled and fell."

Mansa: "Take him away!" Hafeez was seized and taken into custody in a howdah placed on a camel meters away from the Mansa's tent.

Chief priest: "Your highness, the skies above us have changed color and form; we suspect imminent danger from bodies suspected to be darkspirits as well as hellspirits. Let's release the children and avert threats to our people and these people that host us on our way to the holy city."

Mansa: "Let us keep them, the woman who sent them will surely come to get them, then we get her."

Chief priest: "Recall the damage and lives lost when we had alien activities in the city of Maroja, we must avoid any such thing here and now. Also your highness, the boy is crying uncontrollably. We fear he might provoke spirits to come rescue him."

Mansa: "Let us see what happens next."

Chief priest: "As you wish, your highness."

Chapter seventeen
Maroja

Tinuke woke up to substantial changes in the skies; at once she remembered that it signified their mission was accomplished and time to head back home has arisen. She's worried and crying, she wishes to be with Hafeez so the spell can initiate the process of Mkposa and journey back home as taught by the queen.
Tinuke: "Friend, how do I get my brother? The change in the color of the skies mean that he has convinced the Mansa about announcing unready Africa in that loud manner just yet. It's time to leave."

Velus: "Oh mine! I fear they are not intending to release you just yet so they'll hold on to your brother a while longer. I heard this much from my lady's private conversation."

Tinuke: "That may be disastrous for us all as the longer brown skies remain, the weather will become more hostile. I have recited the spell as taught by the queen, yet there is nothing happening. I don't know what to do. I wonder how Hafeez is, has he eaten? Is he alright?"

Velus: "Recite it again, this time let's hold hands; who knows!" So they held hands and Tinuke recited the spell again and again.

Tinuke: "In turns in turns we go
                In turns in turns we go
                Return shall be, then condescension shall cease
                Good fortune it is for them who proclaim to see
                Noble is the heart of the servants, success is their will

It's not working. What should I do? What do I say to my mother? Where would I say I left Hafeez." She wept bitterly while Velus consoled her.

At that time, Velus was in the courtyard in Achunaki's lodge tending to some flowers growing when an eerie old looking man dressed in an old and torn garment came by and greeted her. He had beards over his face which hid his looks.

"Daughter!" He said, "I seek an audience with the girl." He added. "But I do not know you, and neither do I know the girl you seek." Velus responded. "I'm Aliliga, and yes, you know the girl I seek. I hear her agony from my resting place and I come to restore her smile. Tell her I can help her get the boy and help them back to their family." At once Velus thought of Tinuke.

Velus: "But how do I get her to meet you? She's the guest of Achunakis' and she cannot be allowed out of the lodge."

Aliliga: "Search within you and you shall find a way. Extend my well wishes to her." And he walked on by with the aid of a stick. Velus ran to Tinuke and told her all that occurred. They devised a plan and disguised Tinuke as one of the maidservants. She was dressed in black silky gown and had a burqa on. She was escorted to the point where Aliliga told them to meet with him and at the exact time of the evening.

Tinuke: "Elderly one, I seek assistance as to how to leave this era and back to where we came from."
Aliliga: "Very well, I can help; on one condition."
Tinuke: "Name it!"
Aliliga: "Will you let me come with you?"
Tinuke: "The gateway opens for two, my brother and I, I can't help you, unless you know how I can travel with one more person." Aliliga smiles.
Aliliga: "Repeat after me- In turns in turns I go
                         In turns in turns I go
                         Return shall be, then condescension shall cease
                         Good fortune it is for me who proclaim to see
                         Noble is the heart of this servant, success is
my will"
Tinuke: "In turns in turns I go
                     In turns in turns I go
                    Return shall be, then condescension shall cease
                    Good fortune it is for me who proclaim to see
                    Noble is the heart of this servant, success is
my will"
Aliliga: "Repeat it. Louder! Louder! Louder!"

Tinuke's eyes turned blazing hot red, sand particles started lifting off the sandy ground. Velus ran away.
Aliliga: "Say it louder!"
Tinuke: "In turns in turns I go
                    In turns in turns I go
                    Return shall be, then condescension shall cease
                    Good fortune it is for me who proclaim to see
                    Noble is the heart of this servant, success is
my will"
The winds increase and displace objects around the area and then make a circle around Tinuke. The dust also rises and covers her from top to bottom. And when the dust settled, there were on the ground Tinuke's clothes.

The Mansa's procession to the holy city was close to Cairo when an occurrence like a mini-tornado visited. The winds whistled past and were *at speeds as fast as light; dust made thick clouds under the brown skies, this further darkened the place. Dust then came over the howdah housing Hafeez and overshadowed it. Everyone was affected; fine particles of sand rested in the eyes of men and animals making visibility impossible for less than three minutes; the musicians, the maidservants, the warrior-guards, the slaves, the priests were all displaced by the strong currents of the winds. And when the dust settled and a headcount was conducted, it was reported that no life was lost but that Hafeez wasn't in his howdah. He wasn't searched for as his clothes, bangles, sandals, rings, medallion were on the cushion.*

Chapter eighteen
Tagoon hospital, Ikeja.
Sunday 3 May, 2020

6:32 pm

There was a distress call lodged at the Ikeja police department of a missing young girl at the Tagoon hospital. Eyewitnesses suggested it was a kidnap and the police were called in. Two undercover police officers were immediately deployed to the scene. Upon arriving at the gate, the police officers attached to the hospital identified the officials in plain clothes and hinted them for the happenings in the last few hours. The undercover police officers after observing all covid-19 safety protocols entered the hospital premises and proceeded to the vip wing where the incident was reported. As they were approaching the reception, there was a loud whistling of winds and sands. The winds blew and moved objects around, displacing everything. Particles of stones blowing in the winds smashed car windows and windscreens, hospital windows and glasses. Electricity supply was disconnected as the winds brought down cable wires and several explosions were heard. This unusual event lasted about four to five minutes. After all, the officials made their way to the ward where the missing girl is reported to have been abducted. As he went up the staircase he met with the girl's parents who were disorganized and needed counseling. They spoke for a brief while and the officers consoled them even more.

Several other police officers in uniforms were in and around the hospital and then a loud cry was heard from one of the nurses on-call being interviewed by a lady police officer. At once everyone rushed and gathered at the door of the ward where Tinuke was bedridden. Behold, it was Tinuke, asleep under the bed naked. "Oh my gosh, oh my gosh!" Korede was yelling at the top of her voice. She and other patients, medical staff and onlookers were restrained from entering the ward and close to Tinuke. Members of the press were forcefully trying to get into the hospital to cover the story; lots of them were recording and holding interviews in the parking lot.

One of the undercover police officers accosted the investigating police officer and the other officers on ground, "You're a disgrace to the force and to your badge. You got a distress call about a missing child and you couldn't even look under the bed? See all the media personalities here present and you'll have to tell them that the person whom you have declared missing was sleeping under the bed. Perhaps she hid there when the weather became turbulent to protect herself. Now you must grant an interview and clarity as to where she was found should not be lacking in your address to the pressmen."

8:12 pm
Tinuke: "How long were you searching for me?"
Korede: "You've been missing for about nine hours, twenty minutes, four seconds."
Tinuke: "Nine hours only?"
Korede: "Baby it seemed like nine months." Tinuke chortles.
Tinuke: "Mummy, where is Hafeez?"

The end.

Translation-
"Kilode to shey ma'n soro egbin simi, to' de ri pe omo yi wa'n biyi? O'ni owo fun mi, bo ti le je wipe awon eyan wa ni bi."
"Why do you always talk rudely to me, and you can see this child is here, you don't respect me even in front of people"

"Mi'o soro egbin si e. Pa pa, Omo na o'gbo Yoruba.
"I'm not talking rudely to you, besides she doesn't understand Yoruba"

GLOSSARY

abeg: please.

abi: right? - it succeeds a question that usually requires affirmation.

aboki: Hausa language: friend, reference to an acquaintance.

agbero: park luggage attendant.

agbo: bitter herbal drink - medicinal.

alawi: allowance - usually monthly.

amebo: gossip.

anoda: another.

ashey: unknown to me.

asun: spicy smoked or barbecued goat meat.

awoof: lover of freebies, glutton, free-loader.

baf: bath.

beta: better.

bin: been.

bobo: young man, middle aged man.

broda: brother.

chao: food, eat.

coachie: coach.

collabo: collaboration.

commot: leave, remove, out.

confam: confirmed.

conji: sexual appetite, on heat.

dash: charity.

dat: that.

de: am, are, at, is.

dem: them, they.

den: then.

dere: there.

dese: these.

di: the.

dia: their.

diokpa: Ibusa: Ibo language: title - usually oldest male.

dis: this.
don: have, has, ready.
dose: those.
draw soup: okra.
e: it, he, she.
eda: either.
egusi: melon.
eva: ever.
flow: slang: represent anything, describe anything.
fada: father.
fufu: cassava meal – largely processed by fermentation of cassava tubers.
garri: cassava meal – processed by frying.
gas: have to, has to, need to, will.
gimme: give me.
gist: conversation, converse.
haba: exclamation, expressing shock, or disbelief.
how fa: howdy, how are you.
im: his, him, her, their.
jam: meet up.
jand: United Kingdom.
jare: a suffix that creates emphasis.
joor: whatever! please -in a lighter persuasive manner. jonz: fool around, misbehave.
kai: exclamation, expression of shock, disbelief.
kanda: cowhide.
keke: tricycle.
kilishi: dried beef, prepared with peppery spices.
kirikiri: maximum security prison.
kno: know.
lemme: let me.
mama charlie: pounds sterling.
mamiwata: mermaid.
mogbe: Yoruba language: exclamation, expressing shock or disbelief.
momci: mother.
moda: mother.
mpkosa: scatter

mumu: fool.
na: it, it's, is, what.
neva: never.
nkem: Igbo language: my own.
nko: also.
no lele: no problems.
no p: no problems.
notin: nothing.
no wam: no problems/worries
oboi: exclamation, expressing shock/surprise
oda: other.
oga: superior.
oga kpata kpata: most senior superior.
ogbanje: witch, one possessed by a dark spirit.
ogbeni: Yoruba language: mister.
oha soup: Igbo delicacy: a kind of leafy soup.
oloshi: Yoruba language: foolish.
oluwa: Yoruba language: God.
owu de blow: phrase for being broke, out of money.
okpari: Yoruba language: it is finished.
oya: now, okay.
padi: friend, close companion.
panya: morning.
pesin: person.
pikin: child, offspring.
ponmo: cowhide.
popci: father.
ppa: place of primary assignment. (Nigeria National Youth Corps)
promo: promotion.
rada: rather.
sabi: know, knowledgeable, aware.
sef: self, selves, also.
sha: anyway, well.
shakara: styling, putting up some attitude.
shaki: tripe.
shebi: hope.
shuku: hair do, packed up in one.

sidon: sit down.
skippo: captain.
solo: alone.
sotey: until, till.
sumtin: something.
suya: smoked-dried beef, prepared with peppery spices.
tin: thing.
tink: think.
togeda: together.
tok: talk.
tru: true, through.
ugba: spicy shredded oil bean seed.
una: reference to a people; a group of persons. v.i.o: vehicle inspection officer (Nigeria)
wan: want.
wat: what.
waka: walk.
weda: whether, weather.
wen: when.
wia: where.
wich: which.
winch: witch.
wit: with.
wetin: what.
wey: that, since.
yankee: United States of America.
yeye: stupid, useless.
yimu: throw a lip at someone to communicate discontent.
yu: you
yur: your
yur fada: derogatory, disrespectful attack at another, disrespect to one's father.
yur moda: derogatory, disrespectful attack at another, disrespect to one's mother.

Printed in Great Britain
by Amazon